Italian Fever

Don DeBon

Italian Fever
Don DeBon

First Printing
Copyright © 2012 Don DeBon

ISBN 978-0-9881783-1-1
ISBN 978-0-9881783-0-4 (e-book)

Dedicated to the one special woman in my life who convinced me to take up my pen again.

Contents

"I don't understand why you are flying over?" Mia Easton said while watching Crystal walk back and forth repeatedly in her New York City apartment, packing. "Why not take the cruise both ways?"

"Because I can't afford to be away from work that long. You know the 'Dragon Lady'!"

"Oh ... right ... she would find fault with God." Mia said rolling her eyes.

"Exactly."

"You look so great in that swimsuit, wish I did," Mia sighed as she looked towards the floor.

"Sis you keep up with that new liquid diet and you will get there."

Mia scowled back, "Do you have *any* idea how hard that is?!? After a few days I start having cravings ... Pop-Tarts ... potato chips ... chocolate ... then a few days after that the countertop starts looking good!"

"I know Sis, I know. I was there. But it's worth it in it the end, don't you think?" she paused to twirl a bit, then continued packing her new suitcases being careful not to wrinkle the delicate fabrics.

"You just love doing that don't you?" Mia sighed.

"Well, I am so happy it finally fits! It's been a long time, and I told myself I would take this trip if I could ever fit in it," Crystal said as she continued packing.

"Did you buy it that long ago? It looks new."

"Well yes and no. I haven't been this size for a long time. I bought it during a clearance sale, but knew it wouldn't fit. I kept it as an incentive to stick to my diet. I loved the style and shape. And you know red never goes out of style." Crystal winked and continued to grin as she packed another of her new dresses away.

"You do realize that this means war." Mia said as she sat back in the overstuffed blue chair and smiled.

Crystal walked over and sat down in the opposite chair and held her hand. "Sis, it is a war you will win. And then we both will go on a cruise."

Mia's head shot up as her grin widened. "You mean it?"

"Of course I do! I wish I could take you with me now, but I'm sure the Dragon Lady would have our heads with the Anderson account so up in the air."

"Yes you are right there. It's really delicate, he is still deciding and we need to keep him or the agency is going to be in a bad situation with the other two large accounts leaving this month. Well, you enjoy it for both of us." Mia sighed as she looked out the window of Crystal's apartment to the mass of traffic that was New York City.

"Oh I will, but I still wish you were going too," Crystal said as she placed the last item in the suitcase, unzipped the expander to increase its capacity then carefully zipped the whole thing closed.

"Me too. Oh I almost forgot I have something for you," Mia said as she reached into her purse rummaging around.

"Sis! You didn't get me a going-away present did you?"

"Of a fashion." She said with a grin as wider than a Cheshire cat while handing over a little wrapped blue box with a shiny white silk ribbon encircling it.

Crystal took the carefully wrapped package and looked back at Mia with wide eyes. "What is it?"

"Well, I would say it's a present. Why don't you open it and find out?"

Crystal smiled as she tugged carefully at the bow. It unfurled and fell away, then she pulled at the paper. She felt guilty ripping the fancy paper but in the end curiosity got the better of her and the paper was torn away leaving a plain hinged box of the same color. Flipping the top open revealed a small cylinder with a spray nozzle on one side and a push button on the other sitting on a ruby cushion. She laughed picking it up and holding the bottom shaking it slightly in Mia's direction. "Pepper spray?"

Mia's smile broadened. "You bet, a girl has got to protect herself these days. And that is a special type I found. It should freeze them in place a few seconds after spraying. No ill effects other than one wicked headache after. It's something new that just came out and won't hold them for very long. Sort of a knock out gas, but not quite from what I read."

"Oh Sis I love you," Crystal said as she squeezed Mia tightly.

She grinned back. "Of course you do."

"And where on Earth did you ever get it wrapped like that?"

"Oh. Well I thought this deserved special wrapping, so I went down to Tiffany's. They will wrap anything if you give them a few bucks," her smile broadened further as she winked, "if it fits in their boxes anyway, which this does."

"But how am I going to take this on the plane to Italy?"

"Oh just keep it in that box. Everyone will think it's from Tiffany's and they will let you right through. Especially this time of year."

"You thought of everything."

"Don't I always?" Mia said as she squeezed Crystal tightly.

Crystal leaned back in the seat and sighed. "Thank goodness I went ahead with first class so I could stretch out," she muttered. Somewhere behind her, a gentleman snored loudly, much to the displeasure of all. The lights were dimmed, but instead of diving into her e-book to escape, she slipped on her headphones and flipped on the Italian language course. She silently repeated the words, hoping they would stick.

"It would be awful to not know how to ask where the bathroom is when I need it," she thought stifling a small laugh.

The flight attendant tapped her shoulder. "May I get you anything?"

Crystal switched off the course and shook her head. "I'm fine, thank you."

The other woman smiled. "Language course? Italian?"

Crystal nodded. "I definitely want to know a few key phrases."

The flight attendant laughed. "Yes, you definitely do! 'Permisso' means 'with your permission, a bit like 'may I please'. And if you are shopping, many will bargain with you, so start with, 'Che cosa significa questo costo?'"

Crystal grinned. "I just want to make sure I can ask where

the bathroom is."

"Dov'e il bagno?" the flight attendant said smiling back. Another passenger called her away before Crystal could say anything more.

Crystal practiced the phrases before she turned the course back on. The rest of the flight passed quickly, and she soon found herself going through customs. When the security guard pulled out the distinctive bluish-green Tiffany box, her heart sank.

"Signora," the big burly guard frowned, his heavy black eyebrows making a dark line across his forehead, "someone loves you very much. Even we recognize these boxes."

Crystal smiled even as her heart raced. "Please don't open it," she thought then spoke quickly, "my friend Mia gave it to me as a 'Yay I am visiting Italy' gift."

The guard placed the box back inside her bag and waved her through. "We are a very peaceful country, and one open to great adventures and love. May you find both, Signora."

Crystal thanked him, picked up her bag and hurriedly walked away. "Whew! Guess Mia was right. Tiffany boxes were the best at hiding all sorts of surprises!" she thought.

Crystal walked up and down the small streets dreamily gazing at the old historic buildings. She was finally in Italy! She had always dreamed of being here and now her dream had finally come true. Rome was beautiful, and the Colosseum was all that she ever hoped. The last 3 days had been truly amazing. She leaned over looking at a small table full of items as the vendor chatted away in her ear why she should buy his merchandise. Some of it she understood, but most of it sounded like elegant gibberish.

While thinking of what to say, her purse was ripped from her shoulder and a tall man dressed in ragged clothes ran down the street clutching it. "Stop! Thief!" she yelled then paused and shouted "Arresto! Ladro!" She ran after him waving what was left of her purse's strap in her hand. All the hours in the gym had left her in great shape, but the man had a head start and longer legs. "Why oh why didn't I take Mia's advice and get a purse with a reinforced strap?" she thought. She cursed realizing her passport and the money she just exchanged into Euro's hadn't been moved into her concealed belt wallet. The man was getting farther and farther ahead. "STOP! Please, someone stop him!" Crystal shouted again between ragged gasps as she kept on running.

The thief was almost out of sight when he fell flat on his face. As Crystal got closer, she could see another man nearby had pushed the thief to the ground. The thief now scraped and bloodied by the sharp impact to the pavement, got up and ran leaving the purse behind.

Crystal ran up to the tall man who smiled warmly while holding out her purse. "I believe this is yours," he said in a strong Italian accent.

"Why yes it is," she wheezed fighting to catch her breath, "thank you very much." Her breathing started to slow, but her heart continued to race. The man was incredibly attractive, and his simple blue shirt and black pants did nothing to hid his well-chiseled physique. She gazed into his eyes, eyes that a woman could lose her very soul into. She snapped out of the gaze when she realized a crowd had gathered and were watching them stare at each other. It was only a moment, but it felt much longer.

The tall stranger's smile broadened. "I am Riccardo Marino, it is a pleasure to meet you," he offered his hand. Crystal took it weakly, and he shook her hand with a gentle, yet strong grip.

"Crystal Bell, and the pleasure is mine. I can't thank you enough for returning my purse, it would have ruined my entire trip," she spoke quickly and tried to get her heart to slow down as it thumped in her ears and threatened to choke her words.

"Ah, I thought you might be. Although, you don't look like the typical tourist." He smiled and Crystal wished he would quit doing that ... it only made her heart go faster.

"Thank you, I try not to be." She smiled back and wished she had worn one of her dresses instead of a pantsuit. But the corners of her mouth curved up knowing it did show off her newly reacquired shape, and she never could have ran after the thief in a dress.

"Are you staying in Italy long?" Riccardo smiled again. "I would be happy to show you a few places here in Rome and try to make up for this dreadful experience."

"Oh, I don't think it was all that dreadful," Crystal thought smiling, but said "Oh I am only in Rome today. I am on the cruise ship Star Princess and she sets sail tonight."

"That is a pity. I had hoped to show you how wonderful my country is," Riccardo sighed, "but would you join me for lunch? I do know of a good restaurant not far from here."

"Oh I would love to!" she said hoping it didn't sound too forward.

Crystal shifted in her chair as she gazed into Riccardo's dangerous blue eyes. "I can't believe I am here in Italy with this hunk of an Italian," she thought watching his eyes moving back and forth inspecting the menu. She loved this little restaurant already. A small one with a great view of the street. Just a notch above a street cafe, which are so common in Italy. She must have seen fifty in Rome, with only a few days in the city.

"Would you order for me?" she said smiling pointing at the menu as the waiter approached. "My Italian is rather lacking." The waiter had reached them by now and Crystal noticed he was dressed in a casual suit with a short apron around his waist and held a notepad. She smiled at the realization that only in Italy do they still use old-fashioned notepads to take customer orders.

"Yes, of course, if you wish," Riccardo said as he turned towards the waiter. "Avremo Capellni Primavera e Salmone Alla Checca grazie."

The man wrote it down on his pad nodding then turned to Crystal. "And la mia signora, you could have asked me directly." He said with a grin spreading across his face, winked, then walked away giving their order to the chef.

"So what did you order for us?" Crystal said smiling as she sat forward in the chair and propping her chin on her folded hands.

"Just a little pasta with vegetables in olive oil, with garlic sauce. And a salmon fillet with diced tomatoes with a hint of basil," he paused smiling, "I hope that meets with your tastes?"

"Why yes, as a matter of fact I love pasta and salmon, how did you know?"

"I didn't, but I suspected you knew something of our cuisine when you took the time to learn our language."

"Well ... " she stammered, felt her face flush, and hoped that her feelings were not obvious to him, "I wouldn't call it learning your language. Barely coping at best or a failed attempt at worst and I am leaning toward the latter." She smiled gazing down at the cobble stones then looking back up to meet those darn blue eyes again. She shifted in her chair with the sudden gaze and this time her leg brushed against his under the small two person table causing her heart to skip another beat.

"I think you did very well. Your pronunciation earlier when you shouted for help was almost perfect. I have met several who did far worse. To the point that I couldn't tell if they were asking for help or trying to find the nearest restroom." They both laughed.

"At least I am not that bad. I would have hated to have been shouting in the square that I needed a toilet," Crystal said still chuckling

"I am sure you would never face such an indignation. You are too much a lady for that."

"Why thank you," this time she couldn't hold it back and

was sure Riccardo saw the blush in her face. "I am lucky that a proper gentleman heard my call and ran to my aid."

"I couldn't let such a lady leave with an appalling thought of my country now could I?" he said with a wink.

"I'm just lucky you were there and I can't thank you enough. And I hope I am not keeping you from anything."

"Not at all la mia signora, I was waiting for a business associate."

"Oh then I *am*!"

"No, please do not trouble yourself. I already rescheduled to meet him after lunch."

"Are you sure?"

"Yes, I am certain. Besides, you are a far more enjoyable lunch companion. And certainly more appealing to the eye."

"Thank you again," she paused blushing even more than the last time, "do you treat all the women you rescue like this?"

"I wouldn't know, you are my first," Riccardo winked while giving a smile that caused her to blush even further.

Crystal was about to inquire further when the waiter brought their lunch and placed the plates down in front of them on the checked table cloth, then quietly walked away. The portions were rather large, which surprised her, but she didn't say anything. "Wow this looks delicious, but what about something to drink?"

"Not to worry. I dine here often and always order the same wine ... ah here he comes now." And the waiter returned carrying a bottle, proceeded to pull the cork, and poured the ruby liquid into each glass with a deft hand.

Crystal raised her glass, sniffed it then sampled the wine relishing it. It was the best she had ever had and wondered what vintage it was. "Lovely wine. I don't think I have had this one before."

"I am not surprised, it is not a common brand. But I come here enough that they keep it in stock for me," Riccardo smiled as he pushed his fork into the pasta and drew it into his mouth with a well-practiced hand. Crystal tried to be as eloquent with her food but felt that she was failing miserably. Only in her mind though, Riccardo saw nothing other than an attractive lady enjoying her pasta. She wondered who this man was that a restaurant would stock wine just for him. She had a thousand questions but instead stuck her fork into a piece of salmon and said nothing.

The view was wonderful from their table with the sounds and smells of Italy blowing all around them on the gentle breeze. But Crystal kept thinking the view directly across from her was the best.

It wasn't long before they had finished the last of their meal and were gazing in the distance when Riccardo asked, "Would you like some dessert?"

"Oh no thank you, I am quite full. If I eat any more, they will have to roll me aboard the ship," she said with a repressed giggle.

"I find that hard to believe, but then I learned long ago never to doubt a lady." He paused to let another smile grace his face then gazed at the clock tower behind Crystal. "While I hate to leave your company, I am afraid I must."

"Oh yes your business associate." Crystal nodded as they began to rise when she staggered a bit forward and Riccardo leapt to catch her. His wonderful strong arms sent jolts of electricity through her.

"Yes. I need to meet–" his words stopped abruptly as he held her looking deeply into her eyes. She could feel their hearts beating side by side. "Are you okay?" Riccardo gazed at her with concern in his eyes.

"Yes, I had ... a little too much to drink ... I think."

"But you only had one glass."

"Wine always does this to me, it makes me sleep if I get too much. I didn't think one glass would do it though ... it usually doesn't." She looked at her glass again and realized they were larger than the ones she normally used. Crystal silently cursed for not realizing this before. "I will be okay ... honest."

"Okay, but I can't leave you like this! It is my fault, and I apologize deeply." He continued to hold her, concerned she might fall over if he didn't.

"It's not your fault at all. Please don't think that. I will be fine in a minute. Trust me." She said gazing up into his eyes. They called to her heart, pulling at her very soul.

"I shall trust your judgment. But my associate can wait a bit more. Shall we go see a few locations I know of and aren't on any tourist route? If I recall correctly you mentioned not needing to be back aboard until tonight?"

"Yes, and if that is okay. I mean are you sure? About your associate?"

"I am certain." Riccardo called for a car and they got in. Crystal heard he and the driver speaking in Italian when she felt her eyelids getting very heavy and she started to drift.

Crystal awoke with a start and blinked in the dimly lit room. "Where am I?" she thought. Slowly she began to remember her lunch with Riccardo and the wine. She blinked again as the room began to resolve. She could just make out the outline of a strange round shaped window with steel framing on the far wall lit by faint moonlight streaming through the glass. "I must be aboard a ship, but how did I get here?" she muttered climbing off the bed. But as she got to her feet, the room began to spin. "I will *never* drink that much again," she groaned and grabbed the nearby wall to steady herself. She felt around and managed to find a light switch. "Finally!" she breathed flipping the switch and bathing the room in white light causing her head to wince as her eyes snapped shut.

"Ohhh I am never ever going to drink that much again," she moaned holding her head then pushed it up to look around the room. Obviously a stateroom, just like the photos on the cruise ship websites she had been looking at for the last several months. Looking down she noticed suitcases on the floor. "Are they mine?" she breathed and checked the name tag. "They are mine! How in the world did they get here?" Feeling in her pocket, she found the key that was thankfully still there. Opening the bags revealed everything just as she had left it in the hotel.

Crystal looked around again to find her purse on the small desk set against the far wall right below the window. The missing strap proved it was hers, as did a cursory look through of the contents. She dumped the contents on the desk to make a thorough inspection. Glancing through the makeup, keys, passport, ticket, wallet, and a few souvenirs purchased earlier in the day, she found a hand written note on expensive paper.

La Mia Signora,

I hope you can forgive me. You fell into a deep sleep shortly after we entered the car. I did not wish to leave you but my associate called and was pressing for my presence. I payed the driver well to make sure you made it to the *Star Princess* before she set sail. I was certain you would make it as the company is very well-known and one of our best. I also found your hotel key, and I know the owners. They were willing to have your luggage sent on to your room aboard the *Star Princess* before she left port tonight. I couldn't bear it if you were to miss your cruise because of me. Again my apologies for not seeing to you there personally. I hope we meet again very soon.

Riccardo

The room spun again, more chaotic than before. Crystal felt the need for air. She shuffled to the door and pulled it open. The corridor lights were even brighter than her room and she winced as her eyes tried to adapt. Smells of sea air and food wafted through the air which made her stomach cringe. She took a step forward and started to fall.

A man in a white uniform rushed forward to catch Crystal with two strong arms. "Are you all right?" he asked still holding her tightly.

"Yes I am fine. I just woke up and I am a bit woozy," she said looking into his eyes, "thank you."

"You are quite welcome," he said then after looking at her for a moment the expression on his face changed. "Ah, you are the lady that was ill and brought aboard earlier!"

"Yes, I guess I was," Crystal stammered.

"Are you feeling better now?" He asked with a look of concern on his handsome face.

She blinked through watery eyes. "Yes much better. Thank you ... "

"Captain Stronga."

"Ohhh you are the Captain! And I almost fell on you! Not good for my first day aboard," Crystal rubbed her head and sighed.

"Nonsense, you are obviously not yourself. Although, you look much better than you did earlier. Are you sure you are all right? I am glad I happened to be walking by on inspection."

"Yes I am sure," Crystal said as the Captain released his gentle but powerful hold.

"Would you like to dine at my table tonight? That is if you don't have any previous engagements?"

"Oh I would love to! Thank you Sir!" she exclaimed then silently prayed her stomach to be in better condition by then or it would be the world's lightest dinner.

"Please call me Captain, I never liked being called 'sir'. Makes me feel as though I should be telling everyone to swab the deck or something," the Captain smiled.

"Of course Captain. And I would be honored to dine at your table tonight."

"Then I shall see you later ... Miss ... ?"

"Crystal Bell." She smiled as the Captain took her hand.

"Then until later Miss Bell."

"Please call me Crystal. And what time?"

"Certainly, and dinner is at eight. Until then." He said inclining his head slightly towards her then turned on his heel and continued down the hallway.

After the Captain was out of sight Crystal moved back inside her cabin and closed the door. Silently she thought "What does one wear when they have dinner with the Captain?" Glancing at the anchor shaped clock on the wall she realized with a start there was only an hour to get ready!

Entering the bathroom, her stomach jumped from the movement. But when she looked in the mirror she winced as it jumped again from her disheveled appearance. Her hair was a mess, and her clothes looked rather wrinkled and creased. She cursed thinking the Captain had just seen her like this. "Well, I will fix that image at dinner, he won't remember this look." She sighed unfastening her clothes, letting them fall into a heap and hopped into the small shower. The warm water was a godsend as it relaxed her. She was glad for bringing her own shampoo, the complementary one smelled more like medicine than her usual rose petals. She continued to relax, imagining the water washing the wine's bad effects down the drain along with the soap as she rinsed.

Wrapped in a towel, she slowly ran a comb through her hair then proceeded to dry it, styling as she went. When it was dry, she grabbed her makeup case and sitting at the sink proceeded to apply everything in equal measure starting with a good foundation. When certain the Captain would approve and not remember her previous unkempt look, she left the bathroom to get dressed.

Opening her suitcases she selected and slipped into a favorite black silk underwear set, then she pulled out her LBD. She smiled thinking "This should get the Captain's attention." Her careful packing earlier paid off as the little black dress shimmered and flowed, free from wrinkles. Crystal stepped into the dress, pulled it gently into place, and zipped it closed. Walking back to the mirror she smiled at how all the hours at the gym had sculpted her body. Opening another bag she found her black pumps, slid them onto her feet, and walked over to the desk.

Looking at the clock again she realized there was not enough time to switch purses, but her eyes flashed with a thought. Taking out her small Swiss Army Knife she removed a few ragged stitches releasing the rest of the strap and effectively converting it into a black clutch that matched her dress. Upon checking herself in the purse's built-in mirror she spied a wayward hair and tucked it back into place. After finding her key, she closed the purse, and left the cabin hearing the lock click behind her.

Crystal walked along the corridor hearing the pleasant sound of her heels on the decking. At the end of the hallway she found what she was looking for: a map. Studying it for a moment she found the main dining room and the best route to get there. Thankfully, it was only a few decks above. Stepping into an elevator she pushed the button for deck 6 and felt her stomach jump again from the motion. A moment later she arrived at the main dining room. The view was breathtaking with the moon shining brightly through the glass enclosed dome. The main level was actually below and she walked down the large red carpeted staircase passing the gold inlaid glass panels adorning the banister. She saw the Captain already seated at his table, some distance away.

Captain Stronga spied Crystal and stood motioning her to join him. She smiled and approached. "Greetings, Captain."

"Hello Crystal, please join us. And may I say, you look wonderful." Captain Stronga gestured to the seat nearest him as a crewman pulled the chair out for her.

"Why, thank you Captain," she smiled as she took her seat, "I am very thankful for the invitation."

"Think nothing of it, we are always graced by the presence of a lady. Aren't we?" The Captain said as he looked around table seeing that every man was nodding in agreement.

Crystal looked around the table seeing the Captain and his officers all in their black dress uniforms. She couldn't recall sitting with such a good-looking group of men before and her heart skipped a beat at the thought. She did see a few others who must have been other guests with their ladies intermingled with the crew seated at the table. All in exquisite tuxes and the ladies in lovely dresses.

A waiter appeared, took their orders and left heading for a pair of swinging rosewood doors in the far corner of the dining room. Another guest, a Mr. Benton Droverson, also seated at the table took this opportunity to ask the Captain a question that had been plaguing his mind. "Sir, I saw a helicopter approach earlier, and it was very close to the ship for some time. My curiosity is quite elevated. Could you please tell me what that was all about?"

"Yes, of course, Mr. Droverson and please call me Captain. We had a gentleman rent our largest suite shortly before we set sail. Due to several circumstances, he was delayed and unable to reach the ship before we left port. However, he was able to have a helicopter catch up to us and apparently had the training necessary to allow him to board from a helicopter while still in flight, as we do not have a helipad. I am sure you will agree that is quite a feat in and of itself. In addition, we were just in range of a helicopter. Any further and it would have been a one-way trip."

"I see," Mr. Droverson said as though thinking of the situation in a different light, "and is the gentleman here tonight?"

"I am afraid not. I met him earlier to invite him to join us, but he was rather tired and wished to dine in his suite this evening. I am sure–" All the lights went out. For a few moments the room was pitch black until their eyes adjusted to the dim moonlight. People started shouting in panic and the crew took charge calming everyone saying that it was a temporary situation and please stay where they are. The Captain whipped out his phone and switched to the intercom channel. "This is the Captain, status report!"

His phone crackled for a moment as though having difficulty receiving the weak signal. "Captain, the main power supply failed and the auxiliary refuses to engage. We do not know why and the engines have shut down as well. We are dead in the water."

The Captain's eyes narrowed, clearly visible in the glow of his phone's back-light. "Run a bypass from auxiliary to main, that should give us 50% power and I want it done yesterday!"

His phone crackled again, "Yes Captain, we anticipated that and it should be done in a few moments."

"Better be faster than that!" the Captain muttered as the lights came back on. Everyone blinked in the bright light. The Captain jumped to his feet. "If everyone will excuse me

I am needed on the bridge. Please stay and finish your meal. We have power for all important functions and we are in no danger but I do need to find out how this happened. Again please excuse me," he turned on his heel and walked briskly out of the dining room.

By this time the catering staff had begun placing food before everyone. Crystal lifted the sliver cover in front of her revealing a delicious meal. Well, normally delicious. Now though as the smell reached her nostrils, her stomach reasserted itself making the room spin. She slammed the cover back on with both hands.

Mr. Droverson, being seated next to her noticed the reaction. "Is there something wrong with your meal?" He said gesturing towards her covered plate.

Crystal sighed, "No, not at all, at least I am sure it is wonderful. But my stomach was upset earlier and is now complaining at the sight of food. I'm afraid I need to call it a night and head back to my cabin. It was a pleasure meeting you all."

"Ah, yes of course. And the pleasure was ours," Mr. Droverson said standing, as did all the other men at the table nodding. They watched Crystal depart before being seated again.

8

Crystal arrived back at her cabin thankful the elevators were still working. In fact, she didn't see anything that indicated there was ever an issue. That was until she entered her cabin.

It was a mess! All her clothing and other items tossed about out of her bags in a very haphazard way. She grumbled seeing many of her nice dresses on the floor in a wrinkled heap. "Who would do this and why?" she thought. But she didn't have time to consider the situation. The door quickly closed and a strong hand encased in black leather shot out grabbing her tightly from behind. The other held her mouth, keeping her silent.

"Please Miss Bell do not scream. I only wish to talk with you. Do you understand?"

Crystal nodded her agreement. The man removed his hand, and she turned around. "Who are you and WHAT are you doing in my cabin?" she fumed.

I am Agent Mighcrow. I am with the FBI,"he paused the show his identification for Crystal to inspect, "as for what I am doing in your cabin, trying to find out what is going on like you are."

"Okay, and what does that have to do with me and my cabin? And why did you tear the place apart!"

"Well first we didn't 'tear the place apart', I found it as you see it," he paused gesturing across the room.

"Then who did?" Crystal's eyes narrowed at the tall man in a charcoal grey suit.

"We suspect the Italian Mafia or someone working for them," he continued to hold his look, strong, unfaltering, as cold as ice.

"Now *why* would the Italian Mafia be interested in my dresses?" She glared at him putting her hands on her hips and tapped her high heeled foot.

Agent Mighcrow's look softened a bit. "It was not your dresses, or even your items at all. But likely what was hidden among them."

This man was beginning to try her patience. "Look, tell me what is going on here so I do not have to keep trying to pry it out of you."

He laughed. "All right, I must say I have never quite been asked that way before and you are not what I expected. Okay, do you know a Riccardo Marino?"

"Yes I do, and I suspect you already know that."

"Correct, but we don't know the details. Only that you met in Italy, had lunch and he made sure you got aboard the *Princess* before she set sail. But not much else."

"I see. Well he happened to stop a purse snatcher from running off with my bag. Then offered to have lunch. I accidentally drank too much wine and fell asleep in the taxi. Next thing I knew, I found myself here with a note giving his apologies."

"Hmm interesting, and you didn't find anything odd among your items?"

"No, not at all. I did look through everything too. Nothing was missing or extra."

"I see. Well, we would like your help."

"Oh you would? How exactly?" Crystal inquired as she continued to meet his gaze tapping her foot faster in annoyance.

"Well we suspect that if Riccardo has not contacted you yet, he will very soon. Meeting you was probably accidental, but everything after it we suspect a method to his actions. If he does contact you, we would like you to tell us his plans and keep an eye on him."

"If he is all you say, wouldn't I be in danger?"

"Very unlikely, which is why we think he chose you. You are the least suspicious."

"But if I am watching him and telling you . . . "

"Oh don't worry about that, he will never know. And we are not asking you to give us anything that would make him suspicious. Just keep us 'in the loop' as they say."

"And how am I to do this?"

"Well be nice and do what you did during your lunch with him in Italy. That is all. And here take this." He tossed a little item.

Crystal was thinking she was never going to do an exact repeat performance of that lunch ever again, as the object flew through the air. She reached out and grabbed the shiny little button. "Thanks, but what is it?"

"It's a one-way transmitter, tracker, and recall. We will know where you are, and if you press it, you can contact us. Also, if there is a problem, press and hold it for 30 seconds. That will activate the recall and we will come to your aid. I can't imagine the recall ever being necessary, but you have it if needed."

"Hmm okay, anything else I need to know?"

Agent Mighcrow opened the cabin door a crack then spoke

quickly. "Yes, identify yourself when you use it as 'Crystal Resistant'. Then the ones monitoring will know who you are."

Crystal blinked "Are you kidding?" But he was already gone. She looked at the closed door then gazed around the mess that was her room muttered to herself "I must be insane." She carefully looked over each item and while nothing seemed to be missing, she was glad to have packed the small steam iron. Whatever had gone through her room, really wrinkled her best dresses.

After everything was put away Crystal thought about her purse. It was the only thing that they had not searched, but she had looked through it earlier. "Hmmm worth a second look," she thought. Dumping the contents on the desk she saw her passport, the pepper spray Mia gave her, her room key, a few makeup items, her wallet, and a couple other items every lady has in her purse but nothing out of the ordinary. She tossed the purse on the desk and heard a soft thud. A sound a fabric purse should not make by itself "That is odd," she thought.

Picking it up again she carefully felt it over and located a small area that was different on the one side. She managed to open a seam and found between the fabric a piece of plastic about the size of a credit card with the numbers 848395830 on it. Magnetically encoded judging by the three black stripes in an odd pattern. More than one stripe was very unusual for such a card. "This must be what they were looking for," she thought.

Crystal considered using the device Mighcrow had given her, but who was to say he was telling the truth. She decided to keep quiet for now and carefully sealed the plastic card back inside its hiding place. Then after putting everything back in her purse, made a mental note to see about getting another bag at the ship's store tomorrow.

9

Crystal awoke with sunlight streaming through her window. "Morning ... it must have been a crazy dream," she thought. Then seeing the tiny little button device on her desk, realized this was no dream. She stretched and was grateful that her stomach was finally back to normal. Then she thought about the time and looked at the rooms metal analogue clock. It read 8am.

Time for a swim. She didn't feel very hungry and a bit of sun might do her some good. Opening one of the drawers she found her swimsuit, slipped out of her nightgown and stepped into it feeling the silky caress of the fabric as it slowly slid into place. Red, high cut and showing every curve. She smiled as she checked herself in the mirror. Time to give this suit a run. Her smile deepened as she grabbed her short cover-up slipping it over the suit. Then after stuffing her sunscreen, room key, and a few other items into her purse, she stepped into her low heeled sandals and headed up to the pool.

The pool was quiet this early in the morning. Crystal found several lounge chairs ready and waiting. She sat in one, took off her cover-up and leaned back letting the bright sun warm her. "Now this is a vacation," she thought.

"Excuse me, is this seat taken?" a man's voice shook her back to reality. Crystal blinked through the glare that her sunglasses didn't quite filter out, trying to focus on who had spoken. She blinked again as a gasp tore from her lips.

"Riccardo? Is that you?"

"Ah you remember me, yes it is I."

"Yes by all means, join me." She gestured to the lounger next to her. "How did you get here? From your note, I didn't think you were aboard the *Princess*?"

"I was not. I did not think I would finish early with my associate. But when our business concluded, I thought I would join you. I was one of the last to come aboard.

"I apologize for not talking with you sooner, but I imagined you needed rest. You were not well when I took my leave of you." He sat in the lounger and smiled. "Lovely day, I always like to have a swim first thing in the morning. Of course I rarely get to enjoy one with a lady in my company." His smile broadened.

Crystal blushed. "Well I rarely get to have one with a gentleman in mine." She returned his mesmerizing smile.

"I very much doubt that," he said smiling again. "Would you like breakfast? I assume you haven't had any?"

"No, I haven't. But I am not dressed for that." She grinned waving an arm over her swimsuit clad form.

"Ah but you forget they have a buffet here on the other side of the pool deck." Riccardo pointed to the area where cruise staff had just completed their task of laying out a large variety of food on several tables shrouded in white fabric. The ships golden logo was clearly visible on the edges.

"Oh they do? I didn't realize ... " Crystal trailed off as she looked where he was pointing.

Riccardo smiled and jumped to his feet. "You sit here and I will get us something. Okay?"

She smiled. "Okay, thank you. Just a–" But she didn't get a chance to finish before he was halfway across the pool area. She considered shouting a grapefruit would be plenty, but then thought better of it. Just as she was getting up to follow, Riccardo returned with a large assortment of breakfast foods on a tray. "Wow, I hope you don't think I will eat all of that!" she breathed in surprise.

"Not at all. But I didn't know what you would like, so I did get a bit of everything. I know it won't be as good as what we had in Italia, but it should do." He smiled again.

Crystal loved his smile. It sent a chill down to her toes. "Steady girl ... steady ... you don't even know this guy," she thought. "That was very kind of you," she said taking some jellied toast and a cup of tea from the tray.

"A fellow tea drinker I see. I also prefer a cup in the morning. But wine always at lunch and dinner. My family think I am odd though as they have wine with every meal, and of course a cup or two of espresso." He then carefully selected a biscotti and a croissant-like pastry filled with marmalade while sipping his tea. "I have always been a bit of a rouge though and don't really care what they think." Riccardo smiled warmly while taking a bite of his pastry.

"Well I prefer tea, although I do love wine with dinner." She sipped her tea and silently cursed he was married. "What is that you are eating? A croissant? I don't think I have seen one quite like it."

"It's called a cornetti. A favorite in Italia, and I am surprised they have them here. I much prefer fresh to prepackaged, but this is not bad."

Crystal had the oddest feeling she was being watched and

took a slow glance around. But not seeing anyone, relaxed while finishing the rest of her toast and tea. "Thank you very much for breakfast." She looked over to Riccardo, smiled, adjusted the lounger, and lain back.

"Is that all you wish to eat? I thought Americans ate more in the morning than this." He said while gesturing to the small amount she had eaten. "You must have Italian in your veins. We don't eat much in the morning."

She laughed. "No I don't think I do, but a girl has got to keep her figure."

"Ah, I see—" Riccardo's phone beeped with a loud twang. Looking down at the screen he frowned at the caller ID. "I am sorry, I must take this call. My apologies."

"Of course, but I didn't think cell phones would work this far out?"

"Generally, they don't, but there are a few repeating cell towers. I suspect we are near enough to one. Please excuse me." He pressed receive, rose to his feet, and started walking. "I told you *not* to call me now, or ever—" Was all she could hear before he was out of earshot.

Crystal relaxed in her lounger when she saw the Captain walking across the pool a short distance from her. She hopped up and speed-walked over to him calling "Captain! Just a moment!" her arm outstretched, hand waving. The Captain stopped at her call and turned waiting for her.

"Hello Crystal. I hope you are enjoying your time aboard?" He smiled and inclined his head in her direction while keeping his eyes fixed on her. "And I do apologize for last night. I hope it did not ruin your evening."

"I am very much Captain, thank you. And not at all. But I did wish to speak to you about something else."

The Captain raised an eyebrow as he returned to his full height. "Oh?"

"Yes someone broke into my cabin last night and–"

The Captain's casual look quickly shifted as his eyes widened. "What?! When?! Were you injured?"

"No, not at all. I wasn't there at the time. It was during dinner last night. Probably when the power went out."

"I see. That makes sense, the locks are far easier to open without detection if the power fails. I haven't heard of any other intrusions last night and it was such a small window …" He trailed off in thought then his eyes seemed to flash. "I promise you I will look into this personally. Was anything stolen?"

"No, nothing, that was the odd thing. And thank you for your help. Do you know why the power failed?"

"Not yet, we are checking into it. We are back up to full power now though, and will meet our next port of call on time. Nothing to worry about. I do apologize for the intrusion into your cabin regardless, and if you would like to move to another one I can arrange it. We do have an unclaimed suite at the moment, and I would be happy to upgrade you."

"My goodness! A suite? Why that would be wonderful!" Crystal breathed fast trying not to let her excitement show.

"Think nothing of it," the Captain said with a dismissive wave of his hand, "we do all we can for our passengers. I will talk with my purser and he will contact you later today. Now, if you will excuse me, I must be getting back to the bridge." He pointed towards the forward section and began walking before Crystal could respond.

"Oh, of course. And thank you again Captain."

"You are welcome, have a pleasant day."

Crystal turned to look for Riccardo but he was gone. A

moment ago he was a few yards away from the loungers, now he was nowhere to be seen. "Odd," she thought. "Wonder what happened?" She walked back over to the loungers to pick up her purse and found a note scribbled on a napkin.

"I'm sorry. Can I perhaps make it up to you? Dinner at seven in the main dining room? I will be there, hope to see you then."

The note trailed off as though he thought of writing more, then decided against it. Crystal sighed as she picked up her purse and walked back to her cabin. A smile crossed her face with the thought: she had a date for dinner.

10

Crystal thought about the day as she began to get ready for dinner. She watched a comic in one of the small theaters, and shopping in the ship's store. She even found a new purse she liked, carefully transferred everything over to it (including the strange card hidden again under an inside seam), and threw the old one away. She hated to as it was one of her favorites, but it wasn't the same without the strap. This time though, she got a purse with reinforced steel webbing in the strap like Mia had suggested. No one was going to cut and run with her purse again.

The ship's yoga class was great, and she really enjoyed the relaxation and getting a few kinks out at the same time. While there was a full gym, she was not about to work out on her vacation. And there would be plenty of time after.

She also had time to lounge around at the pool for a bit with a book she downloaded to her e-reader while in the ship's store which was really getting good. But then her phone beeped with a reminder of her dinner date.

Back in her room, Crystal slipped out of her clothes and stepped into the hot shower. She had looked through her dresses and decided on a red cocktail dress that ended just above the knee. It hung on the back of the bathroom door, the steam already working on removing a few minor wrinkles that occurred when her room was ransacked. While her new suite did have a deluxe steam iron, this was an easier method. And she really needed a long shower to think.

As the water cascaded down, she thought of Riccardo and how he had disappeared. And why she kept getting the feeling of being watched. At one point she thought she saw a man in a suit, but when she turned, he was gone. She was not sure if it was her imagination or not. The past couple of days could have made her oversensitive, but then again what if she wasn't?

The hot water relaxed her as she lathered up and rinsed off then continued with her hair. Crystal was grateful for the suite upgrade, it even came with a security system, but she still couldn't shake this feeling. As the day wore on she kept the little button transmitter in her hand or pocket that Agent Mighcrow gave her. It helped thinking she could call if there was a problem, and perhaps that who was watching her? Or was it just in her head? These thoughts continued to swirl in her mind as she watched the soap wash down the drain. She wished her concerns would disappear that easy.

Crystal stepped out, wrapped up in a towel, checked that all the wrinkles had fallen out of her dress, and began to style her hair with the suite's ion hair dryer. She was amazed how fast it worked and made a mental note to get one when she got home. Grabbing her makeup case, she applied her makeup while being careful to use just enough to bring out her eyes and complexion.

Pulling her grandmother's pearl necklace from its case she slipped it around her neck. Then placed the matching earrings in each ear. Smiling, she thought "Well, he should do a double take tonight." She slipped on a set of red satin panties feeling the coolness of the fabric as they slid up into place, then donned the matching bra. She took her dress off of the hanger, stepped into it, gently pulled it up and zipped it. She then slipped on her red high heel strappy sandals and fastened them. Pausing a moment to check herself in the full-length mirror, confident all was as it should be, she grabbed her new purse with a removable cover that matched the dress, left the suite, and locked the door behind her. A faint beep as she walked away confirmed the alarm activated.

Crystal sighed as the elevator made a faint ding passing each deck. She checked and could feel the keycard in the lining of her new purse. With the extra padding in this purse, no one would find it unless they knew specifically what to look for. Or so she hoped. The doors slid open to reveal the main dining room and all of its finery. Crystal stepped out and breathed in the faint scents of meals being served. As she walked down the main stairway, she saw Riccardo at a table near the middle corner of the dinning room. One of the more private tables in the room she noted.

A waiter approached from behind her. "Miss Bell?"

Crystal turned with a start. "Yes?"

"Mr. Marino asked me to direct you to his table."

"Yes of course, thank you." She walked fast trying to catch up to the waiter that was already several steps away.

Riccardo looked up from the menu as she approached and stood to greet her. He took her hand and kissed it. "La Mia Signora it is good to see you again. I do apologize for running off so abruptly earlier, I hope you can forgive my rudeness."

"Of course. I knew that something important must have happened. And you have all of dinner to make up for it," she smiled as the waiter pulled out the chair for her and pushed it in after she was seated.

"I plan to do just that." He smiled then gestured to the menu as he sat back down. "I hope you don't mind, but I have already ordered for us."

Crystal's eyes widened. "Oh?"

"Yes, but do not be alarmed, it is a little salmon, ravioli, with risotto on the side. I hope this meets with your tastes? I knew you liked our food, and I thought you would like a typical Italian dinner since I did not get the chance to offer one back in Italia." He said pausing to look around then lean close. "And I happen to know there are very good Italian chefs aboard." He winked in her direction.

Crystal smiled. "Yes that is fine, thank you." But wondered how in the world she was going to eat it all. After a few moments lost in Riccardo's smile she pulled herself back to reality. "You didn't mention anything to drink? I assume you ordered that as well?"

Riccardo's eyes flashed, "Yes of course, how careless of me not to mention it. We Italians always have wine with dinner and I didn't think to–"

Crystal raised her hand. "No need to apologize, that is perfectly all right. Although I hope–"

"It is a lighter wine than we had in Italia? No need to concern yourself, it is only Rosso." He said with a slight wave of his hand.

Her eyes narrowed. "Rosso?"

"A light red wine. But now while our meal is being prepared, the real reason I asked you to join me tonight–"

"There is another reason?"

"Well I do always enjoy your company, and I do wish to make it up to you. However, yes there is, and I wanted you to hear it from me before anyone else. But I suspect you already have."

Crystal blinked. "Oh?"

"Yes. Well let me start at the beginning. Most of my family is not the sort of people you would want to be involved with."

"What do you mean?"

Riccardo sighed. "Well I guess there is no easy way to say this, they are in organized crime."

Crystal blinked and while she knew this was likely what he wanted to tell her, it was still a bit of a shock to hear it from his lips. "You are with the Mafia???" She tried to keep her voice low.

Riccardo leaned closer. "No, I am not. I left them long ago. But they keep trying to get me 'into the fold' I think is how you put it. They always knew I was the most intelligent in the family and want to use me to further their organization. I; however, have other plans and want no part of their illegal deeds."

Crystal sat back and sighed. "I see. It must make your life very complicated."

"Yes, it does at times. But as I said, I want *no* part if it. Some people outside the organization think I do work for them because my family has implied I do. Hoping that it would bring me closer to them."

"Why are you telling me this?"

"Because I think you are being watched. I am not sure by whom but I am fairly certain you are. Have you seen anything out of the ordinary happen?"

"You mean other than my room being turned up side down when I was away? No I–"

"Your room was ...how do you say it ...ransacked? Searched?"

"Yes it would seem so, though nothing was missing."

Riccardo sat back and sighed. "I am sorry, I did not mean to involve you. I only wished to treat you to lunch, then later on I wanted to make it up to you in person for the way I failed back in Italia."

The waiter returned with their meals, carefully sat them down, proceeded to pull the cork from a wine bottle, and poured them each a glass. They thanked him and he said to call if they needed anything else, then left.

Crystal looked at the carefully prepared salmon and ravioli with their wonderful flavors wafting to her nose. She sat back sipping her wine feeling the light refreshing taste in her mouth. Thinking he was right, this is a very sweet wine, she spoke softly, "Riccardo, you have not failed. What happened at lunch was entirely my fault. As for my room, well it could have been someone else. We don't know it was your family. Either way you are more than making up for it." She smiled warmly swirling the wine in her glass although felt the opposite. She did not want to let on that his family was probably aboard. It was obvious he was nervous, no need to make it worse.

Riccardo looked into her eyes, saw the warm smile, and realized he should have known she would react this way. Even with the few moments they had spent, he knew this woman was very different from most. "Thank you, I am very glad to hear that." He smiled back with a look that made Crystal's heart jump and she shifted in her seat bumping his leg with hers under the table causing her to blush. But Riccardo's smile only broadened.

As the evening continued, they found more and more in common and were laughing at the different funny situations they had been in. They were so greatly enjoying each other's company, when Crystal looked at her watch, she gasped. "It's almost 1am!"

"Is it? I had no idea. I have kept you far too long. Please forgive me."

"Riccardo ... please ... there is nothing to forgive. I cannot remember the last time I had such an enjoyable dinner. And it truly has been."

"Oh La Mia Signora, it is I who should be thanking you for being so tolerant of me. And I admit I cannot recall the last time I had such an enjoyable dinner either. But then I do not often have a chance to dine with such a lady as you." He reached across the table to take her hand in his then caressed the top while looking deeply into her eyes.

Crystal blushed as her heart started to race. "Why thank you, but a man like you must meet so many ladies–"

"None like you," he said his gaze never faltering.

She blushed further as another waiter appeared. "I'm sorry but this dining room is closing in a few minutes. We do have many other areas still open, if you would like I can give you a list."

Crystal looked up to the waiter as they withdrew their hands. "No, that is not necessary, thank you." The waiter nodded and walked off. "Well I guess we should go."

"Yes we should, but I must admit I wish the evening was not ending," he said continuing to look into her eyes. Those eyes felt like they were reaching into her heart with a warmth she never thought she would feel. While it was a little cool in the room, her racing heart did not let her feel it.

Crystal sighed softly. "So do I."

Riccardo stood and offered his hand. "Would you allow me the honor of accompanying you to your room?"

Crystal looked up and smiled as she took his hand. "Yes, and it is I who am honored to have a gentleman escort me."

She stood and Riccardo offered his arm. They intertwined and left the dining room.

They talked softly walking the deck and feeling the warm soft breeze as it rustled Crystal's dress. Looking up at the shining stars, they relished in the beauty of the night, and found themselves outside her suite all too soon. Crystal slid the keycard into the lock, then punched in the code to deactivate the alarm.

Riccardo's brow furrowed. "I thought you had a stateroom?"

Crystal smiled. "I did. But the Captain was nice enough to give me an upgrade after the intrusion."

"Ah, yes that was very nice of him," he bent down and kissed her soft lips. It started as a simple good-night kiss, but then it lingered on and he wrapped his arm around her back pulling her close. Crystal's knees went weak, and she saw lights in her eyes. After what seemed like an hour he pulled away. "I am sorry the night has to end," he sighed.

"Who says it has to end?" she said slightly breathless. "Would you like to come in for a few? It's very nice and quite sizable. Probably larger than yours."

"Oh La Mia Signora, thank you for the kind offer, but I couldn't ... "

"Please? I don't want this wonderful evening to end either." She smiled and gazed up into his eyes.

Riccardo squeezed her softly and relented. "How could I say no to that?"

"Well you just did."

He laughed softly. "I did, didn't I? Idiotic of me wasn't it?"

"Yes it was." Crystal smiled and laughed with him as they walked inside. The door clicked closed behind them.

11

Riccardo looked around the spacious suite with its beige carpet, white plush furniture in the living area, and noticed the bed and bathrooms off to the side. The doors were closed blocking his view within. "Very nice," he said with a slight nod.

Crystal smiled. "Thank you. I was quite impressed myself when I got the upgrade. The ship's purser showed me around and how to use the security system. Would you like a drink? I think there is something in the bar area. To be honest, I haven't had time to explore."

"Yes, thank you." Riccardo said as he walked over to the bar. With a deft hand he opened a fridge that Crystal didn't know was there, withdrew a mineral water, and a small bottle of wine. "I didn't think you would want any more wine tonight," he said while holding out the mineral water.

"Yes you are quite correct, I had my limit tonight." She laughed taking the bottle, twisted the cap hearing the pop, then letting some of the clear liquid trickle down her throat. "Thank you."

"I thought as much." He pulled an opener from a drawer, popped open his small bottle, and sipped. "It's not as good as we have in Italia but certainly not bad considering." He smiled again as his eyes gleamed.

Crystal sat her bottle on the bar. "Thank you for a lovely evening."

He put his bottle down, walked around the bar and stood very close gazing into her eyes. "Who says it has to end?" He said as he ran his fingers through her soft hair.

"Riccardo ... don't ... we don't hardly–"

"Know each other? La Mia Signora, I know you are feeling what I am feeling. And neither of us want the night to end. I have never met a lady such as you." He gazed into her eyes and wrapped a strong arm around her waist and pulled her close. Never breaking his gaze continued to move closer until their lips made contact. Lightning sparked between them and Crystal's knees weakened as her eyes rolled back. While in the blur of passion, his other hand slipped behind and gently pulled down the zipper of her dress.

Crystal barely felt the fabric parting as the dress slid down gathering at her feet. When she came back to her full senses, she realized that she wanted him ... badly ... oh so badly. His blue eyes sparked again on his handsome face and she felt the rest of her reserve melt away as he kissed her again with a burning passion few people ever see. She gasped as her knees buckled but his strong arms didn't let her move a millimeter. She reached down and unfastened his belt sending the pants they held straight down to the floor. Grabbing him with both arms around his strong neck she held on tight, as though she was in a hurricane.

Riccardo reached around and unfastened the center clip in the middle of her back. With her soft breasts now free of their confinement, they pushed the bra away. The straps gently, slowly slid off, and the garment joined the others in a heap on the floor. In one fluid move, he took one arm and swept it around behind under her legs into the back of her knees continuing the motion until she was off her feet and fully in his arms. He kissed her repeatedly as he carried her toward the bedroom. Pushing the door open with his foot, he placed her on the bed as though she was the most precious thing in the world.

His shirt and jacket fell to the floor revealing a very muscular build. He was not a young man by any means, but certainly one that took very good care of himself and worked out a great deal. His white boxers glowed in the dim moonlight showing a faint shadow in the front indicating he was very pleased to see her.

Riccardo moved closer and kissed her again, slowly, passionately and Crystal felt the blood thunder in her ears as he moved down kissing each and every inch. Going around and around her feminine mounds loving, caressing and loving them more. Crystal vaguely thought this man is too good to be true as he kissed her again and with a tender hand moved down below causing her to moan this time. Then the same hand removed her panties as though a great treasure was being revealed.

He kissed her again, and she felt her heart skip a beat, perhaps it was several beats, she couldn't tell. Time seemed to stand still. He came closer and closer until she felt something slide inside her and knew it was him. She couldn't recall when his boxers disappeared and didn't care. She moaned as he filled her in ways she never thought possible. Holding each other so very tight as though they were one, and at that moment they were. She moaned and their hearts thundered as they continued to kiss, their insides burning with unrestrained passion. Moving together as one faster and faster. Time slowed again. Again and again ... yet they were moving faster ... as one. Until neither could take any more and they exploded together with the stars in their eyes going nova.

They continued to hold each other and fell back up on the bed still not letting go. Kissing softly, tenderly and gazing into each other's eyes. The sheet was pulled up covering them, but neither remembered who did it as they fell asleep in each other's arms. As they began to drift Crystal wondered if it could get any better than this.

12

The moonlight filtered down in the dark corner of a rarely visited upper deck area. Two shadows approached each other looking around making sure no one had seen them. Then the larger of the two pointed to the concealed doorway, and they stood within its frame. No one would see them unless they were mere feet away. They faced each for a moment as the scents of the sea air wafted, filled their senses. The strong breeze caused their hair and clothing to flap.

"Did you find it?"

"No I am sorry . . . we did check–"

"I don't want excuses! I want results!" Benton Droverson exclaimed in hushed tones careful that no one would hear, but making sure his point was clear. "Keep looking, he must have it. Either him or that woman that was at the Captain's table the other night. I know they had lunch in Italia. There must be a connection. Possibly his contact. Either way *find it!* If you don't, I will find someone else that can, and you know what that means!"

"Yes. We will not fail you," the man said as he inclined his head.

"You had better not. It has the ability to transform this planet as we know it and I must have that power. Do I make myself clear?"

"Perfectly. We will find it. Do you want me to eliminate the woman? It might make him tell us where it is hidden."

"No, that won't work. I know him too well, it will only strengthen his resolve at this point. However, if the proper situation is set up, then it may. Keep that option open but do *not* proceed until I tell you. Is everyone in a position to take the initiative should we need?"

"Yes, all is ready."

"Excellent. I want the plan executed at a moments notice, *but* only if we need. I would rather we maintain a low profile; however, if it becomes necessary ... "

"We understand."

"Good. And make sure you continue communication as I previously set up. And do not contact me again directly unless absolutely necessary. I wish to maintain the current cover for as long as possible. Preferably ... indefinitely. Now go." Benton said with a wave of his hand

"Understood." The man said nodding then looked around to verify they were the only two in the area. "I will do as instructed."

Benton turned back having looked away for a moment, but when his gaze returned, the man was gone. It was as if he had never been there. Which is as Benton wanted. He double-checked the area and went back to his suite via a long route buying a few items from the ships store along the way. If anyone had seen him outside his suite, they would only assume he had a late night snack-attack, including the lady waiting for him in his room.

13

Sunlight started to peek over the horizon gently kissing Crystal's face with its dim but increasing light, waking her. As her eyes fluttered open, she felt a moment of disorientation. Then she took a breath and smelled Riccardo's cologne and realized last night was no dream. She smiled, but it quickly faded as she turned to see Riccardo already awake and carefully walking across the room towards the desk. He reached out, picked up her purse, and proceeded to carefully look through its contents.

Crystal's eyes narrowed, and she sat up quickly. "Find anything interesting?" she said in a flat tone.

"La Mia Signora! You ... you are awake! I ... "

"Yes I am, and what do you think you are doing?" She sat with her arms crossed over her sheet-clad body.

"I ... I ... I–"

"I'm waiting." Crystal stated flatly with her fingers drumming on her arm as her look grew colder still. A look that could make an ice burg cower and run.

Riccardo sighed deeply then walked over to the edge of the bed and sat down with his head in his hands. Sighing again he turned his head, still in his hands, so he could see her. "I guess I should start at the beginning."

"I think that would be a good idea." Her gaze still transfixed upon him.

Riccardo sighed again, straightened and turned towards Crystal. His one leg bent at the knee and moved upon the bed as he turned. "First, I never meant to draw you into this. But I knew I was being followed and there was no way I was going to get out of Italia with it."

"It?"

"Perhaps you found it. At least I hope you did as I know you have a different purse . . . a small odd looking plastic card with 3 magnetic strips on it in an unusual Z pattern."

"I did."

"And you still have it?"

Crystal's eyes stayed stern. "I do."

"Oh thank God," Riccardo sighed with relief. "It is a very special card as you no doubt noticed. It all started a few weeks ago when a friend contacted me. He was very upset and wanted to meet me within the hour. Needless to say it was difficult to meet him on such a short notice, but I cleared my schedule and managed to do so." Riccardo sighed again and leaned closer. "Have you heard of a Professor Croorlheart?"

Crystal paused for a moment thinking. "No, I don't think so."

"I am not surprised, he tried to maintain a low profile. He has done a lot of research into new forms of energy, but not many know that. When I met with Terrance, sorry Professor Croorlheart, he was in a highly agitated state. More than I had ever seen him. He kept looking around as if expecting someone else and spoke of an incredible discovery and that it would change the world as we knew it.

"Then he suddenly looked away again and when turned

back his face was as white as a sheet. I asked him what was wrong, and he said he hadn't slept in days and was being followed. He wouldn't tell me any more as he did not want to involve me, but then why call me and want to meet so quickly? He was not making much sense. Then he looked around one last time and shoved something into my hand, saying 'Keep this for me, and whatever you do, do not lose it.' I looked down at my hand finding that card covered in sweat and when I looked back up he was gone."

Riccardo gazed down at the floor then back up at Crystal who was listening intently. He slid closer to her and took a deep breath. "Three days later I learned that he was dead. An apparent suicide by jumping from the Tower of Pisa. But I know this can't be true for two reasons. One, he was very happy with his research and would not have killed himself. And two, he was afraid of heights. He could no more have jumped from the Tower as I could grow wings and carry him up there. The next day I received an envelope with no return address and in it was a simple cryptic note 'Zero Has it, Please take care of it 453439524210420471RetroEpsilon'."

Crystal blinked. "That is a very odd message. Did you have any idea what he meant?"

Riccardo shook his head. "None. I have been trying to figure out what he meant and what this is all about. I suspect whatever breakthrough or discovery he made that card is the key to it. But how or where to use it, I don't know. And that night my office was broken into yet nothing was missing or disturbed. The following day my home suffered the same fate, and I had the feeling I was being watched even though I didn't see anyone.

"I suspect it may have been my 'Family' but why they would want the Professor's work? It doesn't make sense. I know he would never work for them, even remotely, so that can't be the reason. I am so sorry La Mia Signora, I never meant to involve you. I could not let them find the card, and I knew what ship you were going on. I thought it might be an easy way to get it away from them as they would never suspect you having it. So I slipped it into the lining of your purse after you fell asleep in the car." Riccardo's eyes fell to the floor as he signed again. "But right after, I realized how mentally lacking that was. I never ever should have placed you in danger even if the possibly was remote." Riccardo took her hand into his and he kissed it. "I don't know what came over me, I never should have done that and realized it right after but by then it was too late ... I couldn't bear it if you were to come to harm due to my stupidity."

Crystal looked at him, into his eyes as they came up from her hand and her gaze softened. "It's okay. You were trying to keep the Professor's work away from whoever is attempting to steal it." Then her gaze hardened. "But if you ever try to pull something like that again I will have you feed to the sharks! Clear?"

"Perfectly." Riccardo said as his shoulders slumped.

"And I think they are on to you. Well us."

"What do you mean?"

"Remember I told you my cabin was ransacked while I was at dinner? What I didn't mention, it was my first night aboard. I bet they were looking for the card key."

"WHAT?! HOW?! I can't believe it!" Riccardo gasped. "When you mentioned it before I assumed it was some random thief. How did they find you so quickly? I thought they gave up thinking the Professor must have passed it on to someone else since they stopped following. At least I think they did. I never did actually see anyone, but that odd feeling

I had before evaporated. And that was before we met in Italia. Do you really think it was them and not some normal thief?"

"Well at the time I thought it was, since he had used a ship wide power failure to get in. Now it seems more likely that power issue was created just to find that key. Nothing was missing, but my room was a mess. And are you sure you don't have any clue where it might be to?"

Riccardo shook his head. "None"

Crystal shifted under the sheet as she looked out the window and chewed her bottom lip. A moment later she turned toward Riccardo. "From what you said the Professor was very careful and I think I might have an idea what it goes to."

"You do?" His eyes widened as his mouth fell open.

"Yes. There is a new company called Zero Stor in Switzerland. They have a new automated safety deposit system. The agency I work for did their recent advertising campaign. It's unique in that it is totally automated. Without the key and pass-phrase you can't get direct access to the box. And they do allow deposits of all kinds. All you need to do is print out a special bar-coded label, attach it to the package, and send it. The package is placed in your box automatically as soon as it arrives. I haven't seen one of their keys, but the Z pattern of magnetic stripes on the card looks very much like their logo."

"Very interesting, I hadn't heard of them. And yes this does sound like something the Professor would use."

"I'm not surprised you haven't." Crystal said as she stretched and proceeded to get dressed, planning to take a shower and a fresh change of clothes before they left the suite. "They only went online about a month ago and have not advertised globally yet. We were the first company to get the contract. Do you have the note the Professor sent you?"

Riccardo shook his head as he pulled on his pants. "No I burned it right after I received it. After the circumstances of his death, I wanted to make sure no one else could read it."

"Good. At least we know no one else has that." She said as she zipped up her skirt and fastened the belt.

Riccardo walked over to the window and put his hands on the sill gazing out at the sun now well above the horizon. Something was going off in the back of his mind. A tingling . . . a feeling that he was missing something. He looked back out the window again to the sun and his eyes widened as it came to him. "We are heading south!"

"Excuse me?" Crystal blinked.

"The sun is rising and the only way it would shine in this suite in the morning is if we were heading south! And we should be heading west on this cruise not south!" he exclaimed.

"You're right, why didn't I notice that? Very strange."

"Can you ask the Captain? You seem to know him."

"Yes of course. I am sure there is a good reason."

"Yes, and I hope it is not what I fear," Riccardo muttered under his breath.

14

Crystal let the water flow over her as her mind raced. Was Riccardo telling the truth? What was Professor Croorlheart's discovery? Or was it something else? The card key was definitely to a deposit box at Zero Stor. Perhaps he was just trying to get the card, it seems everyone has been asking about it. And why was the ship heading south? She had far more questions than answers. She stepped out of the shower wrapped in a towel. Sighing she shook her head as she looked thoughtfully at the steam covered mirror. She had to find out if this story was true or something to play upon her sympathy. She wiped the mirror only to jump upon seeing Agent Mighcrow's reflection standing behind her.

"What the hell are YOU doing here?" Crystal said as she spun around and her eyes narrowed. She was glad that Riccardo had left for his own room awhile ago, explaining themselves to each other would have made Albert Einstein's mind reel.

"We hadn't heard from you in several days and I wanted to check that there had not been any developments that we should be made aware of."

"No. None. I will let you know if there is."

"All right." He turned to leave. "Please do keep in touch.

There are dangerous people involved."

"Just a minute."

Mighcrow turned as he left the steamy bathroom and looked over his shoulder. "Yes?"

"I noticed we are heading south. This ship wasn't to take a southern route only a western route."

"Ah, I wondered if you would pick up on that. Good, we chose well. Yes, we are. The reasons are not clear, but it's obvious the course has been changed. We suspect that it has something to do with certain people wanting to delay–"

"Have you asked the Captain?"

"No. A change of course could not happen without the Captain knowing, therefore he must be in on it."

"But perhaps there is a logical reason for the change?"

Mighcrow laughed. "I very much doubt it. This is a cruise ship, and the line is very static in their routes. They do not change them. The company would rather cancel the cruise rather than have issues with customers or risk their safety. It is something they pride themselves on. This could cost the Captain his command."

"An even better reason to ask him don't you think?"

"No. Too risky. I suspect whoever did the change does not want people to know until the last second. And if it was a legitimate reason, the Captain would have announced it by now. Since he has not, it is far more troubling. Don't you get any crazy ideas of asking him. It's too risky. Do you understand?"

"Yes. And I was just wondering ... " But her words trailed off seeing he had already vanished. Strange he would show up like this. Even more so he couldn't wait until she was dressed. A smile crossed her face as she reached for the phone on her desk and dialed. Others might be suspicious of the

Captain but she had learned to trust her instincts, and they told her the Captain was legit. The others she was not sure of but she had seen the Captain's record and she couldn't imagine him in on any plot.

"Purser's office." A voice came over the speaker.

"Yes, this is Crystal Bell. Can you tell me where the Captain is?"

"Ah, Miss Bell. I hope there is not a problem with the suite?"

"Not at all, I just wanted to see the Captain for a few minutes. He gave me a rain check for dinner the other night and I was wondering if he was planning on tonight."

"Oh I see. Well that shouldn't be a problem. He is on the bridge. I can call him for you if you like?"

"No thank you. I will just drop by. I don't wish to pull him away from anything. This will only take a minute, if he is too busy I will talk to him later."

"Certainly, if you need anything else, just let me know. Have a good day." The phone clicked off.

Crystal walked briskly as she climbed up the decks. Dressed in a medium length black skirt, a tan blouse, with her purse slung over her shoulder she kept wondering if she was doing the right thing confronting the Captain. But her instincts had not failed her before. The sun was very bright by now and it was quite warm. Breathing faster she muttered that there were too many stairs and this could double for the gym. No wonder the Captain is in such great shape.

Upon reaching the door she paused a moment then pulled the latch open and walked inside. The bridge was a fury of activity. Screens lit up all around with several virtual displays showing charts and the GPS positioning of the ship to a few meters accuracy. In the center was the Captain leaning over the largest table sized screen showing detailed charts. He pushed a button, and the chart shifted into a full three-dimensional view overlaying a large storm in the center. Anyone could tell he was quite upset.

"Mr. Schmit, why can't you tell me more about this?" The Captain said as he pointed at the virtual image of a massive angry storm.

"I don't know Captain. It does not make sense. We can't seem to get a positive lock on it and get the details you requested."

"Which is basic information!" he fumed. "You should be able to tell me exactly how far away it is, how large and its path. Not to mention the approximate wind speeds."

"I know."

"Well then? What is the problem?"

"I don't know Captain. As I said, we can see it on all the systems. But specific details are not being given which is highly unusual. It is also odd that it appeared almost out of nowhere. We should have more warning than this."

"Quite. And what am I to tell the passengers? Hmm? 'Sorry we have a problem which we can't tell how bad it is, but don't be alarmed even though we can't tell what it is we know what we are doing.' Can you imagine how well *that* will go over?"

"Yes Captain."

"I want diagnostics on all of this equipment and I want it done yesterday. I don't care if you have to put everything on manual and pull them apart. I want to know what is going on here. In the mean time we will maintain this course. While I have my suspicions this is a very odd glitch in our systems, I am not going to take chances either."

"Aye Captain." Schmit turned and started giving orders to the different technicians and other crew.

"Captain? Do you have a minute?" Crystal raised her hand with one finger pointing up.

His eyebrows rose. "Miss Bell? What are you doing up here? Is there a problem?" The Captain asked as he approached in long quick strides.

"Well I wondered about our course. It seems like we are heading in the wrong direction?" She gestured towards the sun indicating was on the wrong side of the ship.

The Captain sighed and pointed towards the door. "If you please?" Crystal nodded, they stepped outside, and he closed the door behind them. She could hear someone yelling something about shutting down first and then turn off the power before their words were cut off. "I figured someone would notice sooner or later. Although I had hoped we would have more time."

"Can you please tell me what is going on?"

"Yes," he nodded then looked around to make sure no one else was in earshot, "there appears to be a hurricane in our normal path. The odd thing is there was no sign of it 12 hours ago." He gripped the handrail tight enough his fingers turned white and sighed. Leaning forward, he placed most of his weight upon the rail as the salty breeze flipped through his hair. "And as you probably know, hurricanes don't appear that fast, or certainly not to the strength this one is. I suspect it's an instrumentation failure of some sort, but as a precaution we are sailing south to avoid it."

"I see."

The Captain released his grip as he turned back towards Crystal. "We should have the problem diagnosed in a few hours, after that I will make an announcement. I haven't yet as people tend to panic. I can't tell you the number of times I hear 'Titanic' comparisons on a regular basis. And I do not wish to reinforce the thought. Certainly when there is no reason to. And please keep this between us as all I need now is a panic to wash through the guests. At the moment only the bridge crew, you, and I know of this."

"Of course. And thank you for telling me. Will this affect our arrival time?" Crystal blinked in the bright sun as the breeze rippled her skirt.

"Not at all. We can increase speed to make up the difference at this point. Unless we have to sail south for a couple of days, then it would be very difficult to make up that much time. But I can't imagine a storm being that large, even if is there. And I am certain we will find the system error and be back on course in a few hours. Can I do anything else for you?"

"Nope. Thank you very much, I shall let you get back to your bridge." The Captain nodded turned on his heel, pulled the hatch open and went back inside. Crystal could hear "Mr. Schmit! I told you I wanted these stations running diagnostics yesterday! Why are these two still–" before the door clicked closed.

Crystal started walking back to her suite thinking her blouse was too warm for her meeting with Riccardo in the main theater for lunch when she stopped. She had a sudden feeling someone was watching. But when she turned, no one was there. She looked all around found no one and thought that it was a sudden breeze that gave her the chill. But she missed that behind two stairways, in a corner, a shadowed figure was indeed watching . . . very closely.

15

Crystal shivered as she entered the large air-conditioned stage-theater complex. The grand room was already nearing capacity. Its checkered carpet and large drawn red drapes on the stage complemented each other quite well. She looked around crescent shaped two floor room. The second floor contained only seats and was a smaller than the first, set back a bit in a tiered type style giving both a clear view of each other. The first floor was set with dining tables and the walls were richly painted with inlays of different sea images. She saw coral, sharks, whales, multicolored fish, and even jellyfish.

Another chill washed through her as she thought the shorter blouse was a mistake but it was too late to go back for another. Looking up and down the tables trying to spot Riccardo, she was startled by the waiter who approached from behind.

"Miss? Mr. Marino is waiting for you at his table, if you will follow me?" He said gesturing towards the tables. The man looked quite elegant with his crisp black and red uniform complete with perfectly clean apron, but lacking any logo of the cruise line embroidered on it. "Odd," she thought, "not your everyday waiter."

"Yes of course, thank you." Crystal followed the tall man and a moment later reached the table located in a private corner far removed from all others. Riccardo stood gesturing towards the chair a moment before the waiter seated her.

"Hello there, fancy meeting you here," she said smiling.

"Yes it is amazing, after all, this is such a large ship and we happen to sit here together at the same time," Riccardo paused then smiled. "You look lovely."

"Thank you." Crystal blushed.

Riccardo looked up at the waiter. "I will have the pasta with the ship's sauce, the seasoned chicken, Italian bread sticks, and a bottle of your Antinori Tignanello 2008 if you have it."

"Ah yes excellent choice, sir. And you are in luck, I believe there is one bottle left in stock." He looked towards Crystal. "And what would you like?"

"Actually that sounds very good. I will have the same, but with POM Blueberry if you have it."

The waiter frowned for a moment then nodded. "Very well, and yes we do." He scribbled a note on his pad. "I shall return in a moment." He walked back towards the kitchen disappearing behind two large elegant wooden double doors on the far side of the theater that matched the rest of the decor.

"Their sauce is not the best, but it is decent. I figure that the wine will more than make up for it. And what is this POM Blueberry?" Riccardo eyed her while cocking his head to one side.

Crystal laughed. "Oh, I wondered if you would ask about that. It's a brand of juice that is largely based on pomegranate but in this case it also has blueberry added. I find it rather enjoyable and it is quite good for you. Don't get me wrong, I love wine, and I will have some of this wonderful bottle you have selected for us. But after our last lunch, I think it is better I have less. And this will supplement the wine quite well."

Riccardo grinned. "Ah La Mia Signora, always thinking ahead. If you don't mind I would like to try some of this POM if you don't mind. It sounds intriguing."

"Of course. I'm sure you will share your wine, how can I not share my juice?" Crystal grinned. The waiter returned with their bread sticks and butter then shuffled back to the kitchen. A moment later the lights blinked then dimmed as the large stage drapes were drawn back revealing a piano. A man in a long tuxedo walked out. Quiet applause could be heard from around the theater as he bowed, sat at the piano, and began playing classical music.

"He is very good." Crystal said as she nodded to the pianist. Another cold draft from the air conditioning blew through the room and she tried to ignore it.

Riccardo nodded. "Yes he is. And from a good family. I had him perform once for us, but I do not have time for such things as of late. I have been wanting to hear him again for some time. It is a surprise to see him on this cruise." He sat back then noticed Crystal's slight shiver. "La Mia Signora! My apologies for not seeing your discomfort earlier." He said standing as he took off his dinner jacket, walked around the table, and placed it on her shoulders. "It is rather cool in here, someone must have turned the system on too high."

Crystal smiled as the jacket was placed on her shoulders and she felt instantly warmer. And not only because of the jacket itself: Riccardo's scent and warmth from it enveloped her, bringing back the wonderful night before. She blinked, forcing her thoughts to the present. "Yes it is. Thank you, I feel much better now."

"You are welcome. I only wish I had noticed sooner."

"Think nothing of it." She raised her hand in a waving motion and smiled.

But Riccardo took her hand in his and kissed it. "Ah but I do." And Crystal blushed wondering how she was going to remove her hand, yet not wanting to. The question was answered when the waiter appeared a moment later placed their plates before them with the still-steaming food, then walked back towards the kitchen again.

"Oh this looks wonderful." Crystal said as the luscious smells of sauce-covered pasta and tender chicken wafted up to her nose.

"Yes, it does." Riccardo said as he sampled some pasta. "Not bad at all. It is as I suspected though, their sauce could use a bit more oregano and perhaps another clove of garlic. But certainly better than many I have tasted." He began to cut a small piece off of the chicken then paused, looking up. "I noticed that the ship is still heading south. I wonder why. I wasn't able to find out anything when I inquired other than 'Everything is fine, don't worry' or something like it. Which sounded like a cover up to me." He said with a wave of his hand.

"Oh I was able to find out," Crystal said as a smile slowly crossed her face.

"You were?! How?"

"I visited the Captain on the bridge. Apparently there is some sort of glitch or problem in the weather alert system. It says there is a hurricane, but the development was too fast for its size and the Captain is skeptical. However, he is heading south as a precaution. He assured me we will arrive in port on time as they can increase speed to make up for the time difference. The bridge was being torn apart when I left."

"Sounds very unusual. But at least the Captain is taking

precautions. I am surprised he did not make an official announcement."

Crystal stabbed another piece of pasta with her fork. "He is worried about a panic, and he expects to have the problem resolved very soon. And therefore no need to alarm the passengers. Regardless, unless something else happens, we will arrive on time anyway."

"True."

The waiter returned with the wine Riccardo ordered and another odd shaped bottle which he also placed on the table. He proceeded to pull the cork and pour wine for them both. "If you need anything else, please let me know." He said inclining his head slightly, then returned to the kitchen.

Riccardo raised the cruise line logo embellished flute to his lips, tasted, and made a sound of satisfaction. "This certainly more than makes up for the sauce." He smiled, which faded a moment later as he sat the glass down. Crystal looked up as he stopped talking and for a second thought that he was entranced by the pianist but then saw the color drain from his face.

"Riccardo? What is wrong?" she asked.

"I just had a terrible thought. What if the people that were trying to get the card key from my office, and that disrupted your room, are the same ones that are sending the ship south?"

"Why would they do that? Doesn't make sense."

"It does if they are trying to delay us long enough to search more. Or take other action."

"But the Captain said that we would not be late," Crystal protested.

"Not yet. Which means it sounds like they are planning something more."

"Hmm, possible. But there are other more effective ways of slowing down a ship than to sabotage the weather tracking system."

"Only if they wish to remain hidden for as long as possible."

"Yes, I admit it's more subtle," Crystal said nodding.

"And that is what these people seem to be very good at," Riccardo sighed. "La Mia Signora, would you please come back with me to my room and spend the rest of the cruise there? I don't like how this is looking and couldn't deal with it if you were to come to harm."

"Riccardo!" Crystal blushed even though she tried not to. "I am honored but I wouldn't want to impose. And besides I am sure my suite is larger, and it does have that security system."

"Please?" He looked deep into her eyes pleading with his own, then took her hand into his without breaking that gaze.

Looking back into those deep blue eyes, her resolve softened. "All right, for now, if it will make you feel better. But shall we at least finish lunch?" She said while gesturing to the table before them.

"Why yes, of course." He said while sampling more of the tender chicken and wine.

16

In a dark corner of the hold Benton shivered. The area was chilled naturally by the cold water and to preserve the items stored here. He looked around to see crates and shelves with items of all kinds, ready to be used.

"I am here, Sir." A voice called from behind.

Benton whirled around his face stormy. "You don't need to sneak up on me! And the next time you do it, it won't be pretty. Understood?"

"Yes Sir." The man in the shadows nodded. Benton could see the change in lighting from the nod but little else to even know he was there. He had to judge by the voice, which he knew very well.

"Status report." Benton demanded.

"Everything is going according to plan. The ship has been diverted. Do you wish us to take full control?"

"No, not yet. Have you searched that woman's room? I know she was somehow moved into a suite."

The shadowed figure shook his head. "Negative, the security system will make it much more difficult to get inside and there is a possibility we will be detected too soon. We wanted to check with you before proceeding."

"Understood. Yes do it. Get in there and search it, but do

not let her know it has happened if at all possible this time. I wish for us to maintain a low profile ... for the moment."

"Is there anything else?"

"Yes, have you searched elsewhere?"

"Yes Sir, we have. In all locations we could–"

"More covertly I hope than the last time?" Benton growled.

"Yes, no one knew we were there. So far nothing."

"Could she have passed it on to someone else?"

"Doubtful, we have kept tabs on her for some time."

Benton looked suspicious. "Are you sure? She might have given it back to Riccardo."

"Negative, we are certain she did not give it to him. He would not still be with her otherwise."

"All right, but find it! We may have to move on to phase two if it is not found soon."

The man in the shadows nodded. "Yes, understood. Phase Two is in place, but will only be activated at your command."

"Good. And Phase Three?"

"Also ready should we need."

"Excellent. Now get out of here and do as I say. And *next* time send your message to me via the proper code! Someone almost got it before I did. Understood?"

"Yes Benito." The man bowed.

"Don't ever call me that here! It's Benton."

"Yes Sir." The figure disappeared without a sound.

Benton sighed and muttered to himself "It's so hard to find good help these days," as he climbed out of the hold and into the warm sun.

17

Crystal walked with Riccardo's arm wrapped tightly around her. She couldn't help but think that his room was a long distance away from the theater, which was odd. Most of the staterooms and cabins were a few decks below in the aft section of the ship, not above and in front. But she didn't mind the walk. It was a long time since a man had been so thoughtful and caring towards her. Still, did he really mean what he said? She vowed not to let herself get carried away by the hormones raging though her shouting *"Trust him."*

No, she was going to think with her mind, and even if her instincts told her nothing was wrong with him ... there was something he was not telling her. Even if they did have a wonderful day and watched several more shows than planned–the juggling act was truly amazing, not to mention the wonderful soprano singer–she was not going to let herself get carried away.

"Only one more deck. Sorry, I forgot it was so far from the theater."

"No problem, I don't mind." Crystal said as the soft sea breeze gently kissed them and playfully pulled at their clothes causing her to instinctively tighten her grip on her purse. "It's a lovely night. And the stars are so bright."

Riccardo looked up and smiled. "Yes, usually they are almost impossible to see, except in the more rural locations of Italia."

"They are difficult to see from my home as well. But when I visit my parents, I always make time to stargaze. There aren't as many lights where they are." She looked up and mentally traced the Big Dipper and realized the ship's course had still not changed.

"That is good you get to spend time with them. In my case ..." His voice trailed off and Crystal knew now was not the time to ask. "Ah here we are just down this corridor."

"But this is the Starline Deck."

"Yes? Is that a problem?"

"Well, the only thing in this section is the Starlight Lounge on the far side and the Super Grand Suite."

"Oh?"

"Yes it's the most expensive room aboard. I have only heard of top celebrities or dignitaries using it."

"Probably true." Riccardo nodded as they reached a large door deeply inlaid with SGS and the ship's logo. Two large men uniformed men, not cruise staff she noted, standing on either side of it.

"Hello Mr. Marino," one man said then eyed Crystal up and down. "Is everything all right?" Crystal turned to look at Riccardo as her mouth fell open.

"Yes, everything is fine. This is Crystal she will be staying with me." He pulled out his card key, inserted it into the slot, and punched in a long code. Both men nodded as the distinct clink of metal could be heard as several large deadbolts around the doors edge slide back and opened.

Crystal realized her mouth was hanging open, and shut it, only to open it again. "This is *your* suite?"

"Yes."

"So you were the man that arrived here by helicopter?"

Riccardo raised an eyebrow. "Yes. But how did you know about that?"

"The Captain told me at dinner. Well he mentioned it. Someone named Droverson asked about it."

Riccardo froze. "Benton Droverson?"

"Yes, I think overheard someone call him Benton as I left."

Riccardo grimaced for a moment. But Crystal caught it. "Shall we go inside?" He gestured towards the door. "After you La Mia Signora."

Crystal nodded as they walked inside with Riccardo closing the door behind them, locking it. She gazed around the room. Crystal thought her room was richly furnished, but it was nothing compared to this. The room was huge with detailed rosewood paneling containing gold inlays of various nautical designs. There were ships, sea creatures, and a few others she didn't recognize right away. The gold appeared to be real, not gold colored paint. The carpet was thick and felt great even through her shoes. She could just see the edge of the bedroom from her position and it was obvious that it contained a king-size waterbed. There were 3 TV's that she could count with a plush, rich sofa or love seat in front of each one.

She continued her gaze, spotting a bar, and what looked like a large screen that could be lowered from the ceiling. "What was that?" she wondered. "Could this room have a HD projection screen as well?" She also noticed a high-powered laptop with a custom logo emblazed on the screen, sitting on the large matching rosewood desk. A cable ran from it to the balcony where a portable satellite dish was unfurled, pointed towards the sky. There were also several closed rooms further down the hallway. "Wow," she breathed.

Riccardo heard. "Yes it is impressive. Much more than what I usually have."

Crystal looked at him and blinked. "Who are you?"

"I have told you."

"Yes but all of this?" She waved her hand around the room.

"Okay, perhaps I did not give you all the details. I did tell you I had my own ideas and left my family, yes?"

She nodded. "You did."

"Well I am in ...how do you put it ...shipping or package delivery. It is one reason why my family wanted my business. I have done very well with it, and other businesses to the point that it is the largest in Italia. And why my family keeps trying to bring me into their organization. I keep a low profile, so most people do not know who I am. And of course shipping is not something that is ...shall we say ...center stage?"

"I see. Well, forgive me but I am more than a little surprised. And here I thought my room was big."

Riccardo raised his hand. "No need. As I said it is not the size I like, I am not ...as you say ...a showman. But this was the last room they had available when I called and I had to be here. I still regret involving you in this."

"I understand your reasons, you couldn't have foreseen all of this. By the way who are the goons at the gate?"

"Goons?" Riccardo looked at her thoughtfully then laughed. "Ohh they are ...personal guards if you will. I had them sent on ahead, I have known both of them for years. While I don't normally bother with such things, after my office was disrupted I changed my mind. I do like my privacy.

"I see."

Riccardo sat down on the large plush couch. "Well, what

would you like to do for the rest of the evening? I think we have movies that can be accessed on these screens. Although, I admit I haven't tried."

"Yes that sounds like a good idea." Crystal said then her eyes grew large. "Oh wait I just remembered all my clothes are down in my suite. I need to go get them."

"I can send one of my men to–"

"No. Thank you but no. A lady does not want another man going through her underwear," Crystal said with a wink. "I will be back in a few minutes, and you can figure out the movie system while I am gone." She turned to leave.

"Yes I suppose not," Riccardo said laughing. "Forgive me, I did not think of that. Would you at least permit me to have one of them go with you?"

Crystal turned back to look at him with her arms crossed over her chest and her foot tapping. "I get the feeling you are not going to accept 'no' on this are you?"

"Perhaps," Riccardo smiled.

"Oh all right. One can go with me. Deal?"

Riccardo laughed again. "Deal." He stood then walked over to the door and opened it for her.

— 18 —

"Are you sure you don't want me to accompany you inside?" Riccardo's guard inquired.

"I'm sure." Crystal said as she inserted her key into the lock and punched in the passcode, then pointed at the keypad. "As you can see the system says everything is fine. I will only be a few moments. Please wait here."

"Okay. If you need help, just let me know."

"I will be fine," she said as the door closed behind her with a soft click.

"So where have you been?" A voice called from the dark.

Startled, Crystal slapped the light switch and blinked staring at the unwelcome outline in her room. She blinked again, and it resolved into Agent Mighcrow. "If you already know the answer why ask the question?"

"Because I was wondering if you would tell me the truth," he said in a flat tone.

"What are you doing here?" she said as her arms crossed over her chest.

"You didn't check in again, and so here I am."

"I told you I would contact you when there was something that needed to be said, *not* before. Didn't you hear me?"

"Yes I heard you, but that is not proper procedure."

"Like I care," Crystal hissed under her breath.

"What was that?"

"Nothing. Now if you will excuse me I need to pack."

"Pack? Are you going somewhere?"

"That is on a need to know basis and you do not need to know."

"I don't need to know? What do you–"

"Now you listen to me! You will get out of this room and not bother me again until I call. Or I won't tell you anything even if I do find something. You got that?"

"Yes."

"Good now go! Oh wait! On second thought, you wait until I leave."

"Why? Don't you think I know how to–"

Crystal cut him off with a wave of her hand. "I don't care *what* you think. I want you to do as I say and wait a few minutes till after I leave. And I don't want to see you again unless I call. Are we clear?" She ran around the room hurriedly placing her items back into their cases. Silently thanking herself for not unpacking much when she switched rooms.

"Clear. But I do have something you might want to know."

"Yes?" Crystal said rather irritated.

"Well as you probably know, the ship is still heading south. While we are not sure as to who, we do know how."

"Oh?"

"Yes, apparently a virus was introduced into the weather system that created a hurricane where there isn't one. This didn't affect anything directly, but it forced the Captain to change course. Now while we are not sure who did it, it must be someone of high level access to add something like this without being detected."

"Yes sounds likely." Crystal said as she placed the last of her items in the case and locked them both shut. "I'm sure you will figure it out, now if you will excuse me." She grabbed both cases and headed towards the door, opened it and stepped through.

"Here let me help you with that." The guard said and took hold of both cases.

"Thank you, they are rather heavy." She said as they started walking. Neither of them noticed the figure departing the room behind them, eye them warily, then disappear.

19

The guard brought her bags into Riccardo's suite then left. Crystal heard the soft click of the lock securing itself with his departure. She found Riccardo hunched over his desk working on the computer. He hadn't noticed her come in.

"Riccardo?"

Riccardo jumped then swiveled around in his chair. "Oh good you are back. I trust no problems?"

"No. Not at all. Did you think there would be?"

"No. I just was checking." Riccardo said as he turned back to the computer. "Feel free to put your things in the bedroom." He jerked a thumb over his shoulder to the hall on the opposite side of the room.

Crystal had a feeling something was up, but knew now was not the time to ask. "Okay. Thanks."

"Naturalmente ... I mean ... of course," he said his gaze still fixed on the computer's screen.

Crystal walked down the hall and found more than one bedroom in this suite. She thought for a moment and decided to take the vacant one and walked inside closing the door behind her. The room was decorated much like the main room with furnishings in blue and red on a tan carpet. The bed was not as nice as the main bedroom, but still far larger than the one in her old room. She opened the drawers and began to unpack. There was even an attached bathroom complete with a tub which she intended to put to good use. She thought about doing that now, but decided against it.

Hanging her dresses in the closet she silently cursed seeing fresh creases, a result of her fast packing. "Dang that Mighcrow ... if it wasn't for him I wouldn't have wrinkled them at all," she thought then stopped. Why was he there? And asking questions when he already knew the answers? Worse, he could get inside without the security system going off. While she knew this suite was far better, it still begged the question ... could he get in here as well? And if he could, could others do the same? A chill washed through her at the thought. She looked around and found a steam iron in the room and set to work getting out the wrinkles as her mind raced.

A few puffs of steam later, every crease had melted away. She wished the Mighcrow situation would do the same. She stopped at the sight of a basket on the sink in the bathroom. What is this? As she looked through the supply of complementary soap and bath products, there was a red pair of panties in a package with the ship's logo on the bottom. Why would they be here? Had Riccardo been planning this the whole time? She heard a soft knock at the door.

"La Mia Signora? Are you all right?" Riccardo said through the door.

"Yes," she called, "be right out." She threw the panties in an empty drawer, walked to the bedroom door, and opened it to find Riccardo's concerned face as he leaned against the door frame.

"Are you sure everything is okay? I mean, I see you picked a different bedroom ... " His voice trailed off.

"Oh no, not at all," she reassured him. "I have nights where I can't sleep and like to read. I didn't want to disturb you."

"Of course." Riccardo nodded as he let out a long-held breath and smiled. "I did figure out the movies. Would you like to watch one?"

"I'd love to. Did you find anything good?"

"There are several choices, not sure what you would like. Push the menu button on the remote then select 'Movies' on the screen, it will give you a list. I will call for room service. I assume you like popcorn?"

"Oh yes, butter with low or no salt if they have it." Crystal walked into the living area and looked around. "Where is the remote?"

"On the table next to the sofa." Riccardo pointed as he picked up the phone and placed a call.

Crystal found the remote hiding behind a lamp and looked through the large list of movies but nothing stood out. She shrugged and pushed the random button under romantic comedy, sank into the soft couch, kicked off her shoes, and curled her legs up under her.

"Find anything?" Riccardo said as he sat down next to her.

"Couldn't decide so I picked random," she said as the movie started. A smile then went across her face as she saw the title screen. "Ohh I haven't seen this in years."

"Nor have I. It is a classic and always makes me laugh." Riccardo smiled.

"Me too." Crystal smiled back. They both were enjoying the movie laughing hysterically when a man opened the main door and entered bringing popcorn and drinks. Crystal eyed him wary of the ease with which he entered, then she recognized him as the same waiter from earlier.

"Ah Emiliano! Thank you for bringing it so fast."

"Of course, Sir. If that will be all for today?" the man responded.

"Yes. And thank you." Riccardo said as the man bowed slightly and departed.

"You know the staff by first name?" Crystal asked.

Riccardo laughed. "Not at all. He is a friend, and I had him sent on ahead with the other two out front. The line let me bring him and gave him staff access. Probably because I rented this room." He said with a wave of his hand, grabbed the large bowl of popcorn, and offered it to Crystal along with a bottle of POM blueberry juice. He smiled. "Yes, I did remember."

"Thank you." She smiled back. A couple of hours later their sides ached from laughter as the turned off the TV. "I haven't laughed that much in quite a while," Crystal said still grinning.

"Nor have I." Riccardo said as he gave her squeeze, then took her hand into his, and kissed it. "Thank you for choosing it."

Crystal blushed. "You are welcome, but ...if I may ask ...what were you working on so intensely when I came back?"

Riccardo sighed. "Well I had hoped to wait until tomorrow to tell you. But I see now is a better time. You remember telling me of Benton earlier?"

"Yes?"

"Well his real name is Benito Giordano. He is behind the large push to bring me 'into the family'. And I suspect he is also the one that had your room searched."

"He searched my room?"

"Oh no, not him personally. But I am sure whoever did, was following his orders. You see, he rarely leaves Italia. Being he is here, means the situation is far worse than I thought. I also suspect he is behind the ship's change of course. While I don't know the details, I assume it is to keep us here until he has everything in place. Whatever his plan is it can't be good. And the longer we stay the worse it will be."

Crystal blinked. "Well what can we do? We're trapped."

"Ah but that is where you are wrong." Riccardo smiled. "You see, I have called for my helicopter to pick us up tomorrow morning. It is something that Benito will never expect. I am sure he thinks they can't reach us. However, since he has changed the course south it works in our favor. If he had waited another day before doing so, we would have been out of range."

"Are we safe here? And are you sure Benton can't know of this?"

"Yes I am sure. He is waiting for something, which is to our advantage. He can't get in here and I have my men outside as well. I used a secure encrypted link to call the helicopter, so again he has no idea." He paused to hold Crystal tightly. "La Mia Signora, I will never let anything happen to you. I promise."

Crystal's heart melted, she couldn't help but embrace him back and kiss his welcoming lips. Riccardo eyes widened for a second, then relaxed. A moment later they made their way towards the bedroom, leaving a trail of clothes in their wake.

20

Sunlight peeked in the window as morning approached. Crystal's eyes fluttered, then snapped open when she reached for Riccardo and found him missing. She sat up with a start, then leaned over to pick up her underwear when she heard footsteps. A second later Riccardo appeared in the doorway.

"Ah, you are awake."

"Yes. How long have you been up? Why didn't you wake me?"

"An hour or two. And I thought you needed it. There is no rush, and I wanted to make sure our plans are in place."

"Our plans?" Crystal said as she clipped her bra, spun it around, and thrust her arms through the straps.

"Yes. The helicopter will be here in a couple of hours by my estimates."

Crystal looked at the clock "About 9:00 then?"

"Yes. I took the liberty of ordering us breakfast. Emiliano should be here soon."

"Oh, thank you. I think I will get a shower while we wait." Crystal got up and headed to her bedroom.

"Of course," he said then grinned. "Mind if I join you?"

"Not now ... but later ... definitely," she said over her shoulder while closing the bedroom door.

Crystal slid out of her clothes leaving them in a pile on the tiled floor and hopped into the shower. The water felt wonderful and drove the last remnants of sleep from her body. "What a night." She thought as she grabbed a bottle of soap and heard Riccardo turn on the TV in the other room. Not having him waiting outside the door relaxed her. His hovering outside the door was making it difficult to wash . . . alone.

Riccardo sat flipping through the channels on the large projection screen TV. Hundreds of channels and nothing of interest. He turned it back off and was about to check his computer when Crystal walked in. She was wearing a green teal dress with a low V neckline and medium healed golden sandals. He sucked in a breath for a few moments, then realizing he was holding it let it out slow in a very quiet "*Wow.*"

"I take it you approve?"

"La Mia Signora, you look wonderful. Far beyond mere approval."

The door locks slid back and Emiliano walked in carrying a large tray filled with an assortment of breakfast items. "Emiliano!" Riccardo called. "Perfect timing. Leave the tray over on the table. I will call if we need anything else. And thank you."

"You are welcome Sir." He sat down the tray. "I watched everything as you wanted. It should be fine." He paused as he walked past Riccardo whispering in Italian "This lady is nice, you had better keep her." He winked and continued on. Riccardo smiled at the comment and sat down.

Crystal smiled back. "So he thinks you should keep me?"

It was Riccardo's turn to blush. "La Mia Signora! You

heard? He didn't think you would hear, let alone understand. He meant no–"

Crystal grinned. "Riccardo it's fine. I took it as a compliment."

Riccardo let out a huge breath. "Shall we eat?" He said while grabbing a biscotti, a couple of cornetti pastries, and poured them both a cup of tea.

Crystal nodded as she bit into a bagel then took a sip of tea. "What shall we do after breakfast? A little shuffleboard on deck?" she said with a wink.

"I would advise against that at this point. What do you think about a nice movie instead?"

"Sounds good to me." She added another bagel, and a strip of bacon to her plate, then grabbed her tea and walked over to the couch. "What would you like to see?"

"Doesn't matter to me. I am sure anything you pick we will both like," Riccardo said with a shrug. He joined her on the sofa, activated the large projection screen, watched it slide down from the ceiling, then handed her the remote.

Crystal looked through the selections for several moments before finding an old comedy that neither one of them had seen before. Both of them laughed and held each other close. Near the end of the film Riccardo got up to check his computer which had beeped.

"Good news the helicopter is on time. It should be here in 30 minutes. By the way, while I think you look stunning, I think it is best if you change."

Crystal's eyebrows raised. "Oh? Why is that?"

"Well, the helicopter is not going to land on the ship. As you probably noticed, it does not have a helipad."

"Then how is it going to pick us up?"

"By harness. They will lower a cable, we hook up and be lifted off."

Crystal's eyes widened. "Are you serious? I don't know if I am up to that!"

"You have to be, it is the only way we can leave without Benton being able to stop us. I don't know what he has planned, but it can't be good. We need to get off and as soon as possible. Besides, I have done it, it is not hard. It is far more difficult to land than it is to be picked up. And I will be there to help you."

Crystal sighed. "All right, I will try."

"Good." Riccardo smiled as he put his hand on her leg.

Crystal turned off the screen as she got up and headed to the bedroom, then stopped. "What about my luggage? Is the helicopter going to take that up as well?"

Riccardo shook his head. "If we had time yes, but we don't. Once it gets close enough, Benton will know something is going on. We won't have the time as he will try to stop us. We must be lifted off as soon as possible. I will have my men send everything to you once the ship docks. Have it all packed and ready for them to do so."

"I see," she said frowning. "While I thought this cruise was going to be an adventure, I didn't quite picture this."

Riccardo laughed. "I didn't quite plan it this way either, and it will be fine I promise."

Crystal nodded as she closed the bedroom door behind her and began packing. Looking through her wardrobe, for once she silently wished she packed a pair of jeans. But she did find a fairly strong pair of tan slacks, a matching short sleeved top, and a pair of padded strappy flats that would have to do. She opened her purse, making sure that everything she needed was in there, added a few other items, and zipped it shut. A few moments later she was dressed and ready just in time to hear a knock at the door.

"Crystal? Are you ready? We have to head up a deck in a few minutes. The helicopter will be here soon."

"Yes I'm ready," she said opening the door finding Riccardo wearing some kind of harness. "My bags are right there," she pointed, "let them know."

"I will," Riccardo nodded. "Do you have the card?"

"Of course." She raised up her purse.

"Good. Here is your harness." He held out up a piece of clothing that was made out of super strong nylon webbing. "Step into it here," he paused a moment to point out the leg holes, "then pull it up over your shoulders, zip it up, and I will snap the clasps."

"Okay." Crystal stepped in and pulled it up. It didn't look right at first but Riccardo helped adjust the straps so they fit. He pulled up the second zipper, buckled the secondary straps, and made sure her purse was secure in the webbing.

"There," he said smiling, "I think we are ready." In the distance they both heard the faint sound of air beat by fast spinning blades. "It is here, we need to hurry. I am sure someone will hear that and being this far out to sea will wonder what is going on." He unlocked the door, hearing the clank of the deadbolts as it opened.

"You to know what to do." Riccardo said as he gave his guards the suite key.

"Yes Sir, we will catch up with you later. Good luck." The one guard said as he shook Riccardo's hand.

Riccardo nodded grabbing Crystal's hand as they bolted for the deck above. It wasn't even a deck, but rather a small maintenance platform above the suite and the highest point on the ship. By this time the helicopter was close enough for them to feel the strong wind of the beating blades, smell the exhaust raining down on them, and it was starting to get difficult to talk over the roar of the engine.

"Are you ready?" Riccardo shouted.

"No," Crystal shouted back, "but I will do it anyway."

"They are lowering the cable. I will hook it to your harness and they will activate the winch pulling you up. Then it will lower back down for me. You don't have a thing to worry about." Riccardo shouted as the cable lowered. He was about to connect it to the large reinforced ring on Crystal's back when sparks flew off of a rail very close to them. Riccardo turned to see a man holding a gun straight at them. He knew they were sitting ducks in this position. There was no cover, and if they ran, there would be no second chance at this. He couldn't imagine how the man missed unless the strong wind threw off the bullet's trajectory. Benton only hired the best and a second shot would not miss.

The man's eyes narrowed as he squeezed the trigger. Then he flailed his arms as he went horizontal and was tossed over the side to the water hundreds of feet below. Crystal saw one of Riccardo's guards waving.

"GO! We will take care of this!" He shouted then turned to see another man running up the stairs, an obvious backup. The guard flung himself in a tackle maneuver taking them both out of Riccardo's view.

"Okay!" Riccardo shouted. "Change of Plan!" He grabbed her from behind hooking the large clasps of his harness with her own. He waved upwards with an okay gesture.

"What?" Crystal shouted back, but he didn't have time to respond as the helicopter took off at high speed, yanking them skyward.

— 21 —

"I thought you told me he couldn't get a helicopter from this distance!" Benton fumed then looked up to see one of his men nodding indicating the storage area was indeed secure.

"That is what I was told." A shadowed form replied.

"You know the penalty for failing me." Benton waved and a large man with a stern expression approached.

"Sir! I am more valuable to you alive! And it was not I that failed you, someone else told me the distance was too great."

Benton thought for a moment. "You might be correct ... I may have further use for you. Still, someone must pay for this failure."

"I will take care of it. Have I ever failed you?"

"True. All right, I shall let you take care of it, and let me know when it's done."

"It shall be." The shadowed figure bowed deeply. "And what of the men he left behind? Shall we proceed with phase two as previously planned?"

Benton chewed his lip. "No. He would not have left them behind if they knew anything. Riccardo is too smart for that. I should know, I trained him."

"Yes, Sir." The man bowed again.

"And since we are in range, I want a helicopter here

tomorrow to pick us up. There is nothing more to be done here."

"Are you sure? I can have others follow them."

Benton stuck his finger in the man's face. "Do NOT question my orders! Yes I am certain, I would have not said so otherwise. And I am not leaving this to anyone else."

"I will have it here tomorrow." The man bowed deeply.

"Good. Do you know where they are going?"

"No, but we can follow them."

"Excellent. This situation may yet be saved. Along with your life." Benton growled.

"I shall not fail you."

Benton pointed at him again the redness in his face fading starting to fade. "You had better not. Or you will not get the chance to ever make another mistake."

"Understood."

"I will not lose this!" Benton paced the room back and forth then paused looking back to the shadowed figure. "Croorlheart betrayed me and I will not lose the discovery. I should never have left him alone for so long, but he insisted the progress would be faster."

"You could not have known–"

"I should have. But never mind I will have it in the end. Or everyone in this room will regret it. Am I clear?" Benton growled.

A quiet unanimous "Yes," was heard from several areas around him.

"Good." Benton said as he started climbing out of the ships hold. "Now I don't want to hear anything more until that helicopter is here tomorrow. You have caused enough commotion that I am surprised a general panic not was generated. Yes we could take command of the situation, but at this point it would be useless." Benton said as he finished climbing out of the ships hold to the deck above and into the warm sunshine.

Crystal shut her eyes as she dangled from the cable and felt the vibration as the winch slowly pulled them in, all the while praying it didn't snap. A moment later strong hands pulled them both inside the helicopter and shut the door.

"That was a heck of a risk," the pilot said edging the controls forward, trying to coax more speed. "You know the cable is not approved for that much weight."

Riccardo took a moment to catch his breath then shouted still a bit winded. "It couldn't be helped." He grabbed Crystal's hand as he unlocked the part of the harness holding them together. "Are you okay?"

"Yes," she shouted finally opening her eyes, "or at least I *will* be."

The other man handed them two headsets. "At least now we don't have to shout." Riccardo said as he squeezed her hand once more then turned back to the pilot. "How are we doing?"

"Pretty well considering Sir. We should have enough fuel to reach an alternate air field. I just hope we don't hit a head wind."

"You and me both," Riccardo turned back to Crystal. "Get comfortable, it is going to be a couple of hours before we land.

Don't worry Marco is the best pilot in the business. We will get there."

"And where is that?" Crystal asked still looking a little pale.

"Marco, can we reach Jerez?"

"I am afraid not Sir. But we should be able to reach Faro without too much trouble."

"Good that will do." Riccardo nodded then looked towards Crystal squeezing her hand. "Better rest, I have a feeling we will need it."

"I will try," Crystal said as she squeezed his hand back.

"I had hoped to reach Jerez as I have more contacts at that airport. But Faro will do. I trust you brought your passport? We will need it when we land in Portugal."

Crystal's eyes grew wide. "Portugal?"

"Yes, we can't reach Spain as I had thought, but we can reach Portugal."

"I don't know any Portuguese," Crystal sighed.

"Don't worry, I do," Riccardo smiled. "Just get some rest. We will be there soon."

Crystal didn't know how she managed to doze off with all that was going on, but the steady engine vibration and ongoing beautiful sea scape view out the window gently lulled her to sleep. She woke as the landing struts kissed the tarmac in Faro.

"Good job Marco" Riccardo said as he grabbed his shoulder. "We can take it from here."

"Thank you Sir." He pointed to the gas gauge. "It was close though. Thankfully, the wind was only fighting us the last few miles, the meter is reading empty as it is. Do you want us to wait here?"

"No, get refueled and head back. If I need you again, I will call."

"Yes Sir. Good luck."

"Thanks," Ricardo nodded as he and Crystal climbed out of the helicopter. "Over there," Riccardo pointed. "I have a car waiting with a customs official. Hand him your passport, and we will be on our way in a few minutes."

"No problem," Crystal said then stopped and raised her hand. "Wait where are we going?"

"Zero Stor of course." Riccardo smiled. "I checked it out last night while you were away. As you said before, it is obvious that the Professor's keycard is from there. The car will take us to the other side of the field where I have my private plane ready for us."

Crystal's eyes grew wide. "Private plane?"

"Yes. I called ahead right after we got into the helicopter and had it flown here." Riccardo said as he gestured towards the black car waiting for them a few yards away. "Shall we?"

"Yes we shall," she said as they began walking towards the car. They were almost to the door when a man emerged smiling.

"Good day Mr. Marino. I am Alfonso Aguiar. Welcome to Portugal. I trust you have your passports?" the man asked in Portuguese.

"Yes," Riccardo responded. "But can you speak in English? Miss Bell here does not know your language."

"Ah of course. My apologies," Alfonso said in a very thick accent. "May I have your passports please?" They both handed him their passports which he checked in detail. "Very well, everything is in order. May I ask how long you plan to stay in Portugal?" He asked as he stamped both of their passports and handed them back.

"Only an hour or so. I have my plane here ready to take us to our next destination," Riccardo responded.

"Of course," Alfonso said. "As I suspected. But I had to ask, regulations you know."

"Yes, certainly." Riccardo said shaking the man's hand. "Thank you again for your assistance."

"You are very welcome Mr. Marino. Always happy to oblige. Enjoy your *short* stay in Portugal and please do call me if I can be of assistance," Alfonso said as he began walking towards the terminal.

Crystal stared at Riccardo. "Just how many people *do* you know?"

"A few. But it does come in handy at times as you can see." Riccardo laughed as they got into the car and rode across the airport to the private hangers.

"I do indeed." Crystal said as she watched the driver take them to one of the larger hangers where she saw a long sleek jet with a blue streak down its side and up to the tail. She blinked in surprise. "Is that yours?"

"Yes it is. One of my vices I guess you could say, I hate to fly coach. And too often had problems even when flying first class. Also they never seemed to have a departure time when I needed." The car pulled up, and they both got out Riccardo stopping to offer his hand and help her out. "Pietro should be ready for us."

"Pietro?"

"My Pilot," Riccardo said as they climbed the stairs and into the jet. There at the entrance they found a tall man with broad shoulders wearing a black uniform complete with aviation wings. "Pietro! Good to see you," he said shaking his hand.

"Good to see you too Sir," Pietro said with an Italian accent. "We are all ready to depart."

"We have clearance already?"

"Yes, I made sure of that as you mentioned we are in a

hurry. If you take your seats I will start the engines and taxi out of the hanger. We should be in the air in ten to fifteen minutes."

"Excellent. Pietro, this is Crystal."

Pietro paused raising his fingers to his aviation cap's front edge and inclined his head. "Nice to have you aboard Miss. Please take your seat, and if you need anything you have but to ask." He nodded to Riccardo and headed for the cockpit.

Crystal paused to look around the most lush jet she had ever seen. The red carpet was thick and she could feel her feet sinking into it. The walls were paneled in a low golden color with wooden accents. She saw a bar, several seats that looked more like loungers you would find in a house and even a sofa alongside one wall. And what looked like a room in back with a closed door. All told it was larger than her first room aboard the *Princess*. "Wow," she breathed.

"It is nice isn't it? I do admit I might have went a bit excessive when I furnished it, but as I said I do call it my vice. However, it has paid for itself in not having to spend time through the security checks."

"That I can imagine," Crystal said nodding. "The checks are terrible."

"Yes, not to mention I do not like the idea of having radiation scan my body several times a month. They say it is safe, but I have my doubts." He pointed to one of the plush seats. "You will find the straps along the side. There is a flap here and here you pull open to reveal them." Riccardo said as he made sure she was properly secured, then did the same for himself.

Riccardo clicked the intercom. "Pietro, we are ready."

"Yes Sir. I just contacted the tower, they have verified the runway is clear and we can take off immediately."

"Good, then do so."

"Yes Sir. Here we go." Pietro said as he fired up the two massive engines. Crystal could feel the vibration as they started, then smoothed into a slight background drone by the time they started heading for the runway. A few moments later they were in the air.

"We have reached cruising speed and altitude Sir. Estimated landing in Zurich is three hours."

"Excellent. Let me know if there are any changes."

"Of course," Pietro said as the intercom clicked off.

"What shall we do for three hours?" Riccardo said looking towards Crystal.

"Well, I would like to freshen up if you don't mind. That helicopter made a mess of my hair." Crystal sighed.

"Of course. It is in back." Riccardo gestured towards the door in the rear section then pulled out a laptop from a storage compartment. "While you do that, I am going to check a few things online."

"You have a connection up here?" Crystal blinked.

"Of course, satellite link. May not be the fastest method, but in general works quite well."

Crystal unbuckled the strap and headed to the rear section. But when she slid the door back her jaw dropped. There was a large, plush, comfortable bed that matched the rest of the decor, a dresser, and along the far wall another door which she assumed would be the restroom.

"My my aren't we full of surprises," Crystal said over her shoulder.

"What? Oh the bedroom. Well there are times I would rather sleep here than in a hotel, especially one I don't know. Much simpler. And I did tell you I may have gone ... um ... overboard as you say. The bathroom is in the back, but go easy on the water. I don't have much stored right now to save weight." He turned back to his computer.

Crystal walked to the second door and opened it finding a super-light tub-shower combination, sink, mirror, and a closet with fresh linens. She realized her mouth was hanging open again, and she made a mental note to stop doing that as she closed the bathroom door. She really wanted a shower but settled for a sponge bath instead since she didn't have fresh clothes, anyway. A little later she emerged feeling much better and her hair was no longer in the 'wind blown' style.

"Find anything interesting?" She said leaning in the doorway with her arms folded across her chest.

"Hmm? Oh." Riccardo said spinning around in his chair. "Yes. My men aboard the ship are fine. I wasn't sure what Benton would do. Apparently after we left, he lost all interest in them. I also was getting directions from the airport in Zurich to Zero Stor. It is a relief they are close.

"Yes they are. Although I have not been there, it was part of the advertisement campaign not being far from the airport and very convenient for international travelers." Crystal said as she sat down again and pulled out her e-reading device from her purse. "At least this gives me time to finish this book I had started up on the pool deck."

"Or we could watch a movie," Riccardo grinned.

"Oh? You have movies here?"

"Yes via the satellite link. There isn't a huge selection as I don't use it often. But we might be able to find something."

"Sounds good." Crystal said putting her book down then looked around. "Where is the screen?"

"In the bedroom. It lowers from the ceiling. Shall we La Mia Signora?" He said offering his hand.

"Yes we shall," she said smiling. A few moments later they

were curled up on the bed as the large screen lowered and the image was projected on to it from a source hidden behind them. They picked an old black and white classic, *The African Queen.* She sat back resting comfortably against Riccardo. Soon they were into the movie and forgetting all about the current issues.

23

"Why isn't the helicopter here yet?" Benton growled.

"I don't know. They said they would be." The man in the shadows said. "But don't worry they won't reach their destination."

"What? What have you done?!" Benton almost yelled.

"I ...I ...I arranged for their plane to be *adjusted* so they wouldn't reach their–"

"You did *what*?"

"I ...I ...thought you would be pleased."

"Pleased? PLEASED?! Do you have any idea what you have done? If that key is destroyed we will never get access."

"But I–"

"Silence! You have failed me for the last time." Benton said with a wave of his hand. A microsecond later the very tip of a large blade was sticking out through the shadowed man's chest causing him to look down in shock a moment before Mr. Schmit fell over quite dead.

Another man straightened from behind. "I never did like him. I'm not sure why you took him on."

"We needed the access at the time. Now that his usefulness is done, so is he. I hope that he did not destroy our chances to get the key," Benton muttered through pursed lips.

"I doubt it. Riccardo is very ... resourceful. I suspect whatever Schmit did, they will be able to divert to a closer airport. If anything, it will make it easier for us to catch up," he paused noticing a faint engine drone in the background, "and I think your ride is here."

"Yes, I believe you are right. Take care of this." Benton paused to indicate the body on the floor. "I would prefer the crew not know what happened for awhile. And are you riding with us?"

"Of course, consider it done." The shadowed figure bowed. "And no I am not. The helicopter will travel faster without me. I will find my own way."

Benton nodded. "As you always do. And be sure to keep in contact."

"Don't I always?" The man smiled.

"That you do ... that you do." Benton said nodding with a slight shiver as he pulled on his harness and left the cold storage area heading up to meet the helicopter.

24

The intercom buzzed. "Sir?" Pietro said in his thick Italian accent. "I think we may have ... a ... problem. Can you come up here?"

Riccardo frowned as he clicked the intercom. "I will be right there." Then turned towards Crystal. "I will be right back. Don't go anywhere." He gave a wink as he walked towards the forward section.

"Don't worry I won't," she said smiling, "and I will pause the movie for us."

A moment later Riccardo leaned over Pietro who struggled with the controls. "What is it?"

"I do not know. The controls are stiff and sluggish and our fuel consumption is extremely high. It happened all of a sudden."

"Can we make Switzerland?"

"I don't see how. I think we can make EBU."

"St Etienne, France? That is only about halfway!"

"I know Sir, I wish I had better news. But at this point I think we may be lucky to reach St Etienne. And even then, I don't know if I can land there."

"Why not? They have a strip large enough."

"Yes they do, but they had an accident there earlier today and they are waving off all planes our size and above."

"I thought they had a second landing area?"

"They do, but not for a jet of our–"

"Could you land on the smaller one anyway if they would let us?"

Pietro thought for a moment still fighting the controls, his knuckles white. "Perhaps, it would be tight even in normal circumstances. One thing is for certain we can't take off from there."

"At this point as long as we can get down in one piece, I will take it." Riccardo looked over the navigation system and then the maps. "Do we have any other airports in range?"

"I don't think so Sir, unless you want to count a large grass field as a landing strip."

"All right make for St Etienne. Better radio ahead and make sure they will even let us try. But they should if we declare an emergency."

"I hope so." Pietro muttered with an intense look as he continued to fight with the controls then clicked his head set to transmit, dialed in St Etienne's frequency and advised them of their situation. His face was grim when he looked towards Riccardo. "They will let us land, but will charge us for any damage to the runway or their facilities. Also they said due to the other accident their normal emergency response systems are drained and cannot offer normal assistance should it be needed."

Riccardo rolled his eyes. "Great. They are not expecting us to live are they?"

"Given our size, no. Sir, I suggest you and Crystal jump before I land. We do have parachutes in the back."

"I won't leave you to–."

"You must! It is bad enough if I die ... but if I take my passengers with me when there is an option? I cannot have that!"

"All right," Riccardo sighed, "thank you my friend. But I know you will make it."

"I wish I was so certain." Pietro said as the controls began to bounce even more wildly. "You had better go tell Crystal."

"Yes." Riccardo said as he grabbed the pilot's shoulder they both nodded towards each other letting what they were feeling go unsaid.

"La Mia Signora, we have a problem." Riccardo said taking her hands in his. "The plane is having serious control issues and there is a fuel loss on top of that. We do not know the cause."

"Can we land?" Crystal said her eyes wide.

"There is only one airport in range given our situation and they do not have a functional runway large enough for us at the moment."

"What are we going to do?" Crystal squeezed his hand tightly.

"Pietro is going to try to land on the small strip. It is questionable even in the best of conditions. But we are going to jump out before the plane–"

"Jump out! Are you crazy?" Crystal exclaimed.

"We have parachutes. And it is more to case him than us. He doesn't want us aboard when he tries to land."

Crystal sighed and squeezed his hand again. "All right but just so you know, this will be the second time in 24 hours you have messed up my hair. And I am going to send you the bill for my hairdresser," she said with a wink.

Riccardo laughed. "Well considering you could bill me for more, I think I am getting off easy." He said winking back at her as he went and opened storage area. But upon pulling out the parachutes he frowned. "These have been tampered with!"

"Tampered with?" Crystal walked over to him as the plane shook and groaned causing her to grab a seat for support.

"Yes. See here?" Riccardo pointed to the plastic seal over the pull cord. "We always have seals put on the chutes when they are tested twice a year. A certification of sorts to know they are in good condition. These seals have been broken. Someone tried to carefully piece them back together but I can see the separation point," Riccardo opened chutes and frowned more after inspecting them. "Well no wonder! Several of the lines have been partially cut. They may hold given the short distance we are to use them for. But I doubt it."

"Then what do we do?"

Riccardo looked up and took her hand again. "Looks like we are in the for the ride of our lives."

Crystal squeezed his hand in hers and slipped him a kiss. "Ever since I have met you, it has been the ride of my life."

Riccardo smiled as they went to the cockpit hand-in-hand.

Pietro looked up at them. "Why are you not wearing your chutes?"

"Sabotage." Riccardo looked at him his face blank.

"Sabotage?" Pietro questioned.

"Yes, the seals were broke and the cords have been partially cut through to make it look like an accident."

"How is that possible?" Pietro blinked.

"I don't know. But they are. Can I help you here?" Riccardo pointed to the co-pilots seat with an extra set of controls. "I do have flight experience you know."

"Yes you can. Sit down and strap in. Okay, grab the controls and be ready ...engaging in 3 ...2 ...1 ... *now*."

Riccardo held tightly as the control yoke fought hard bucking and bouncing in his hands. "Wow. She is really fighting."

"Yes. But it is better with your assistance." Pietro clicked on the radio and switched it to speaker so all could hear. "This is flight 289 from Faro en route to Zurich. We are declaring an emergency as previously stated. We are on approach and should be landing in an estimated 5 minutes. Please clear the runway."

The radio crackled with slight static that dissipated. "This St Etienne flight control. Please be advised we cannot guarantee the runway will be clear by then. Please circle around for another approach."

"Negative control, we do not ...cannot do that. Controls are sluggish, fighting, and fuel is low. Recommend you try to move everyone you can off of that runway as we are coming in, if we want to or not."

The radio hissed back. "Understood. God be with you."

"God be with us all." Pietro prayed. "We are on approach. I want you to drop the gear when I say. We can only drop them at the last minute, can't afford to lose any power beforehand. And whatever you do, work with me." Pietro checked his instruments then frowned. "Our angle of approach is off. Turn five degrees in 3 ...2 ...1 ... *now*."

"Confirmed." Riccardo said as they turned the yokes in unison. The controls continued to bounce wildly and fight them every second. "And there we are," he said once they were flying level again. "Crystal strap yourself in, there is a fold down seat right there. Or use one of the seats in the back. Either way I want you strapped in."

"I was about to ask if I could use this one here. No way I am going to be wandering around now." She said squeezing his shoulder as she flipped the seat down, locked it into place and strapped in.

"Ease it down ... gently. Throttles down. Flaps down."

"Done and done." Ricardo said flipping switches. The plane was shaking more than before, the fuselage groaning louder, and even bouncing making them wish their stomachs could have been left in Faro. Suddenly an alarm went off.

"Dang!" Pietro shouted. "We just lost an engine. Adjust trim full right and *pray*." The plane shook even more violently, the sound was almost deafening making them all wonder if the plane was going to fall apart. "Okay here we go ... gear down ... *now*!"

Riccardo flipped the switch as they felt a sudden push forward with the dramatic drop in air speed. "It is down."

"I can tell. All right here we go, pull back *hard* when I say and cut the engine back to twenty-five percent ... ready ... *now*."

Riccardo and the Pietro pulled back hard as they could on the yokes as the plane shook enough to dislodge some dust in the cracks of the consoles.

"MORE!" Pietro shouted. "WE NEED MORE."

"Pulling as hard as I can!" Riccardo shouted back.

Crystal noticed some rope at her feet that was in one of the emergency kits that had popped open. She had an idea. Quickly grabbing the rope she threw it so it landed behind both control yokes in a U shape and pulled as hard as she could with both hands.

"That is doing it!" The Pietro shouted. "Touch down in ... 5 ... 4 ... 3 ... 2 ... 1 ... *now*!" They hit the pavement hard slamming them hard against their restraints. "Brakes!

BRAKES! FULL! NOW!" He shouted again. "Full reverse thrust now!"

Riccardo jammed the thrust lever back, and they were again slammed into their restraints. "Full reverse on. But it is not enough!"

"It had better be!" Pietro shouted. "The hydraulics are all but gone!"

"Look!" Crystal shouted as she pointed to the window. "There is a building at the end of the runway!"

"Yes, I saw!" Pietro said still frantically adjusting controls trying to slow them down more while pushing as hard as he could on the brakes.

The plane continued to roll closer and closer on the short strip not designed for them. It shuttered as they ran out of pavement and began digging into the soft soil. The forward landing gear could take no more abuse and gave out with a loud CRACK. The plane fell down hard still pushing forward, digging a huge trench in the dirt. Control panels fell down all around with the sudden motion leaving them to swing and spark from damaged cables. The smell of fried electronics filled the cabin. Closer and closer they slid towards the large storage building only to end up kissing it before stopping as the remaining engine gave out.

Sparks flashed all around as they shook with the realization they made it. Riccardo was the first to speak. "That was far too close."

"No kidding. I never ever want to do that again," Pietro said.

"Umm." Crystal interrupted biting her lip. "Don't you think we should get off of this as soon as possible? I mean couldn't it still explode?"

"Not likely. We ran out of fuel. There shouldn't be enough

left in the tanks to light a match, much less explode," Pietro said. "But you are right, we should as a precaution."

All three unstrapped, opened the outside door flipping the emergency inflation ramp, and slid down on it. For the first time they saw the damage to the aircraft and Pietro shook his head. "I never had anything happen like this Sir. I am sorry to have ruined your jet."

"Pietro do not worry yourself. It can be fixed or replaced. You; however cannot." He put his hand on the Pietro's shoulder. "I will let you supervise here and get her operational as soon as you can. Crystal and I will continue on to Zurich. Okay?"

"Yes Sir ... and thank you." Pietro smiled as Riccardo and Crystal walked towards the emergency vehicles racing in their direction.

25

A lone helicopter shook again violently over the Atlantic as the pilot fought the controls.

"Can't this thing go any faster?" Benton growled.

"The engines are redlining as it is. I dare not do anymore." The pilot said his voice wavering.

"Do you have your satellite phone?"

"Yes ... it should be–"

"Give it to me!" Benton yelled.

The pilot nodded and opened a compartment then produced a phone with a large antenna. Benton smiled. "Good this situation may yet be saved." He said as he dialed fast. "You hear me? Good. Yes, I want you to do as we discussed before. I am about 30 minutes from Faro. We have a report the Riccardo made an emergency landing, nothing more than that. I didn't give Schmit enough credit. I suspect Riccardo is fine though, he is too smart not to be. Are my reservations in place? I want to take off again as soon as I land in Faro. Good. I will call again when I land." The phone clicked off.

"Everything okay?" The pilot asked.

"Okay? Okay?!!!! We may have lost our one chance thanks to some incompetent fool! Thankfully Riccardo is smarter than Schmit so I suspect they are only slowed down. This may work to our advantage in the end. I have a plane chartered to Zurich we will find and follow them with discretion this time. I will not be denied!" Benton snarled.

A short time later, the helicopter landed with a man in a dark suit meeting them at the pad. The black coat couldn't disguise his large muscled frame. The air swirled around them as the blades spun down forcing them to raise their voices more than they would have liked as they walked towards a large car.

"Update! Any changes?" Benton almost shouted over the drone of the helicopters engines.

"Nothing more. We know they made an emergency landing at St Etienne–"

"Did they make it?" Benton asked quickly.

"By all accounts ... yes. The plane was damaged, but the report is everyone got off of the aircraft without incident," the man said.

"Did they take off again? Or take another plane?"

"No. The plane was damaged as I said, and the main runway at the airport is closed at the moment."

As they reached the car, and the man opened the door for Benton. He moved towards it then stopped and stared in thought for a moment. He turned back towards the man. "A rental car?"

"Yes we suspect so. Nothing definite but it was the only way he could have left the airport. He couldn't have one of his cars there, it is not his normal airport. And the only person still in St Etienne is the pilot," the man said.

"And is the plan I spoke to you on the phone about in place?" Benton said as he got in the long black car. The leather seat squeaked as he adjusted his powerful frame.

The man nodded. "It's in place. Our contact responded only a moment ago to confirm."

"Good. Then we shall know soon enough. Get me on the next plane. We need to be in Zurich."

"Zurich? Are you sure that is where they are headed?" The man said with an eyebrow raised.

Benton looked up at him with his eyes blazing. "Do not question my orders," he said in a sharp tone. "I know where they are going. That was their original flight plan. Riccardo wouldn't file a flight plan for Zurich when he could have gone so much farther in his plane if needed. And we will be there waiting for them."

"Yes Sir." The man said as he closed the car door and tapped on the hood letting the driver know to take Benton to the terminal. The car rolled away as the man got into another car, pulled out his phone and dialed making a mental note he had never seen Benton so impatient.

26

Crystal's nose wrinkled at the smell of jet fuel. There was no doubt this was an airport rental car agency. The only problem was the selection ... there wasn't one. And Riccardo was making that abundantly clear ... repeatedly.

Riccardo walked around the small car as he looked it up and down. "You can't be serious?! It is a scatola di pranzo!"

The Auto Europe salesman blinked. "I am sorry ... a scatola ...?"

"Sorry, I meant this is a lunch box, in reference to its small size."

"Ah, I see. I am sorry monsieur, this is all that we have at the moment. We don't normally have this much demand. If there was anything else I could do, I would," the salesman sighed.

"Well ... " Crystal looked over the tiny two-seater and kicked a tire. It was the smallest car she had ever seen. The only good part she could see was the bright cherry red color. "It should get good gas mileage."

"Yes, if the wind doesn't carry it away first," Riccardo spat. "All right, we will take it. If nothing else, we can exchange it for something else in Switzerland."

"Very well, monsieur." The salesman pulled out contracts

for Riccardo to sign. "Standard contract, you are responsible for any damages and agree to return it with a full tank of petrol."

"That shouldn't be too hard, one drop and it will be filled." Riccardo muttered as he signed the papers then climbed in, adjusted the seat back as far as he could, and turned the key. It started right up with a sound stronger than he expected. "Well at least it sounds better than it looks."

"You will find this has the latest engine designed to give a lot of power for its size. And of course great petrol per kilometer." The salesman said as he headed back to the office, then stopped and turned back. "Will mademoiselle be driving as well?"

"Me?" Crystal blinked. "I don't have a driver's license here."

"You have a license in the states, yes?" Riccardo smiled.

"Of course," Crystal nodded.

"Well that should be enough."

"Monsieur is correct. I only need to see a current license from your country." The salesman said as he held out his hand. Crystal fished out her drivers license and handed it to him. He paused for a few minutes then handed it back. "Thank you, all is in order. Appreciez." He departed walking back to the office.

Riccardo smiled and turned to Crystal revving the engine. "Going my way?"

Crystal smiled back. "Hmm, my mother always said to never get into a car with a strange man."

"But we know each other now." Riccardo winked.

"Oh okay, well then that is different." She said with a wave of her hand and hopped into the passenger seat.

"I think we can make Grenva in an hour. From there it

should be straight to Zurich. At least Saint Etienne is right next to one of the main motorways." Riccardo said as they pulled out of the parking lot and headed away from the airport.

Crystal pulled out her e-reader, but put it away a few moments later when she realized this was a wonderful opportunity to see the French countryside. Something she never thought she would see. But after twenty minutes the sights all looked the same, and she pulled her book back out.

"We are almost to Geneva."

"Already?"

Riccardo laughed. "Yes already. I think I could have run off of the road and you wouldn't have noticed with your nose in that book. Must be a good one."

Crystal stuck her tongue out. "All right, all right, I will put it away."

They soon pulled up at the boarder and had their passports checked.

"Everything appears to be in order," the official stated. "How long will you be staying in Switzerland?"

"Only a few days."

"Very good. Enjoy your time in Switzerland," he said as they were waved on.

Later in the hotel, Riccardo kept looking out the window. "Is there a problem?" Crystal asked.

"I don't know. I hope not. It was the way the hotel owner kept looking at us, gave me an odd feeling."

"Well I doubt many customers come in without any luggage and ask where they can buy clothes. I was thankful they would let us use the hotel's machines to wash them."

"Yes, and I think he bought the story about the airline losing our luggage. But still, there was something ... " He trailed off in thought then shook his head. "Never mind, I am being paranoid."

"Funny, I am usually the one with that problem. I must be rubbing off on you." Crystal winked.

"La Mia Signora, you can 'rub off on me' all you like." He smiled as he headed to the bathroom. "I need a shower."

"Just don't take all the hot water. I want one too." Crystal smiled as she turned on the TV flipping between channels and sighed at the selection. TV was the same all over the world, rarely anything good on. Then her heart stopped as she stared at the screen. "Riccardo!!" she shrieked.

"What? What is wrong?" He ran out and stood there dripping on the white carpet with a towel wrapped around his lower half. "Crystal?"

She couldn't speak only point at the screen. Riccardo turned to see their pictures on it. "Dang it. I always knew Benton had contacts, but I didn't know they extended quite this far. No wonder the hotel owner was looking at us strange."

"What are they saying? My French is not very good."

"They are saying to contact Interpol if anyone should see us. This has to be Benton's work. I need to find a laptop, I can probably clear this up if I can. In the mean time we can't stay here."

"Where are we going?"

"I am not sure, but I am certain the hotel owner saw this and has contacted Interpol. They are going to be here soon. I will get dressed and we will head out. Pack up everything." Riccardo said as he went back to the bathroom.

Crystal sighed packing her new clothes containing several dresses and separate sets along with a nice set of black flats. She also had purchased a new pair of sneakers. She sighed looking at her current pair of flats, they were scuffed after kicking that tire. Crystal silently cursed that it was stupid and lucky she didn't break a toe. Everything was packed when Riccardo reappeared.

"Ready?"

"Yes, but where are we going?"

"Let's try the other side of the city, hopefully no one will recognize us there yet."

"But if they have us all over the tv ... "

"Don't worry, the photos they have of us are not very clear. I am sure if we wear hats and sunglasses, we won't have a problem." Riccardo smiled. "Trust me, most people won't look too close. Also, we have suit cases and clothes now and look more the part of tourists. I suspect he wouldn't have noticed us if we had our suitcases at the time."

"You are probably right." Crystal said as they left the room and went down the back hallway that was opposite of the main desk so they wouldn't be seen leaving. A short while later they found another hotel on the other side of town and Riccardo was right, they never gave them a second look. Although Crystal felt like she was going to rob the place in the dark sunglasses and a large hat she was wearing.

"Of course you realize ... this is the third time you have messed up my hair today." Crystal smiled sweetly.

Riccardo laughed as he turned the key in the lock to their room. "My, I must be racking up quite a bill there."

"Yes indeed," she said still grinning, "and I intend to collect."

The room was not as nice as the other hotel, rather spartan and no TV. But neither of them felt like watching it anyway. Crystal started heading towards the shower grabbing her suitcase. "My turn," she said smiling. The water felt wonderful and at least this shower had a massage option. She turned it on full force and sighed. It had been quite a day, and she was finally able to relax. The hotel soap and shampoo left much to be desired, but she had picked up a nice brand when she was shopping earlier. She came out with a towel wrapped around her head and wearing a mid-length red nightgown.

Riccardo looked up from his laptop and whistled. "Very nice. Feel better?"

"Ah, you approve?" She said smiling, then spun around to give him the full effect. "And yes much better. Thank you. Will that laptop do? I know they didn't have much selection at that electronics store."

"Yes, it will work. I am thankful we found one still open this late," he said then looked back to his screen. "I am not sure how he managed it, but Interpol is definitely looking for us. I have contacts that should set this right, but it might take a few days. I am glad we are already in Switzerland, or we wouldn't have made it this far."

"What do we do now? Stay here?"

"No, I think it would be best to keep moving. We should continue to Zurich. It will be harder to find us there, and we can go to Zero Stor as we originally planned."

"Won't they be looking for us at Zero?" Crystal asked.

"I doubt it. The authorities certainly won't be. There is no way Benton would tell them to go there as it would interfere with his plans."

"But Benton could be there."

"It is possible, but again doubtful. Without the key, Zero won't do anything, so no point in going there. From what I have read, they pride themselves on privacy and discretion."

"They do." Crystal nodded.

"All right let's get some sleep, or at least try to, and we

will start out first thing in the morning. I wanted to get the car exchanged, but the fewer people we deal with between here and Zurich, the better." Riccardo closed the laptop and climbed into the double bed.

"Let me dry my hair first, I will join you in a minute," Crystal said heading back to the bathroom. She dried her hair then crawled into bed falling asleep in Riccardo's strong arms.

27

Light streamed in the open window with the sun gently peeking over the horizon. Crystal stirred and her eyelids fluttered open. She looked up seeing Riccardo's sleeping form still wrapped around her and tenderly kissed his lips.

Riccardo's eyes snapped open. "Morning." He smiled. "I must say that was the nicest wake up call I have had in a long time."

"Glad I could oblige." She smiled and gave him a squeeze.

"I will go get us some breakfast. We should be going as soon as possible," Riccardo said as he got to his feet and stretched.

"And I will get a shower."

"Need any help?" Riccardo winked.

"Not now, but perhaps later." Crystal grinned and winked back.

"Promise?"

"Perhaps," Crystal's grin widened.

Riccardo dressed quickly while Crystal hopped into the shower. Later she heard the front door open again and thought that was really fast as Riccardo had only been gone a few minutes. But something was wrong, he didn't say anything. She carefully stepped out of the shower leaving it running and opened the bathroom door a crack. A man stood inside the room looking around ...and it was not Riccardo! Instinct kicked in and she and knew what to do. She wrapped a towel around herself, grabbed the large ceramic top of the toilet tank, and peeked out the open crack again. He was still there. The tan pullover and tight-fitting jeans he wore did nothing to disguise his muscular build. He stood with his back to the bathroom door, scratched his head ...then turned around!

Crystal pulled her eye back from the door and hid behind it just as the door pushed open. She bit her lip, holding her breath. The man entered and as soon as his head was past the door, she whacked him hard with the ceramic rectangle. He went down in a heap. Seeing the man on the floor and not moving, she finally let herself breathe. But then she heard something outside. She silently cursed. Of course he would have backup. She raised her weapon again, but lowered it when Riccardo's head appeared. "Oh Riccardo!"

As he looked down at the man on the floor, Crystal leapt into his strong arms. He held her tight, then looked into her eyes. "Are you okay? What happened?"

"I heard the front door open and figured you couldn't be back this quick, so I peeked out and found him looking around our room. I hit him when he came in here," she said shaking.

"I saw him enter as the elevator doors closed, so I came right back. Thank God you are all right, I feared the worst." Riccardo bent down to check the fallen form at their feet. "He will be out for some time. I don't know who he is, but certainly not police or hotel staff. Might be a thief that thought the room was empty as Benton's men are far more careful. Either way I will tie him up and we will be long gone before he regains conscious." Riccardo dragged the man out of the bathroom and sat him in one of the chairs using twisted sheets to secure him to it. "This will hold him for now. Finish your shower, I will stay out here and watch him."

"Okay," Crystal said embracing him again, "and thank you."

"Thank me?" He laughed. "You are the one that took care of him, and quite well I might add. Remind me not to get on your bad side." And looked into her eyes smiling as he squeezed her.

"Who knows, you might like my bad side." She said playfully heading back to the bathroom as she removed her wet towel and threw it, seeing it land squarely on Riccardo's face with a solid *whap* as she closed the door.

Soon they were checked out and on the road again. Crystal noted that Switzerland's scenery was far more interesting than the section of France they had just traveled through. A little over an hour later they arrived at Berne and she pointed at the various old buildings with great interest as they stopped for gas.

"I wish we had time, I would give you a proper tour."

"You know Switzerland that well?"

"Well, I have been here quite a few times, yes." Riccardo grinned. "But of course I haven't seen everything. Now Italia, that is another story. I can show you every town, every location in great detail." His grin widened further.

"I would love to have you give me a tour." Crystal smiled back. "Perhaps after this?"

"It's a date then," Riccardo said as he squeezed her hand.

Crystal caught him frowning as he looked in the mirror after they left Berne. "Problem?" she asked.

"I am not sure. The car behind us was at the same gas station we were."

"What is so unusual about that? Probably also had to stop as well."

"Perhaps, but they have stayed four cars behind us for some time. It is probably nothing." Riccardo shrugged. But an hour later the same car was exactly four cars behind them while others had turned off or went past. "Very strange."

"That car still back there?"

"Yes."

"Are you sure it's the same one?"

"Most definitely. He has one damaged headlight," he said as they approached Zurich. Riccardo made sure to turn on the exit at the last second. Crystal watched the car whizzed past them, hit their brakes hard, leaving a trail of rubber on the road and began to back up on the motorway. Cars honked their horns and either slamming on their brakes or trying to dodge the obstacle at high speed. All while it continued backing up. A second later, the driver jammed the loudly complaining transmission into forward and tore after Riccardo down the exit ramp.

"Well that proves it, they are following us." Riccardo said as he got off the exit and headed for one of Zurich's larger roads. "No one would take such a risk otherwise. Hang on, I am going to try to lose them. Make sure your seat belt is fastened." Riccardo squeezed her hand and slammed down on the gas peddle forcing them to be shoved deeply into their seats with the sudden inertia.

28

"You missed the turn off! He took the exit! We can't wait until the next exit or we will lose them!" The man in the passenger seat said pointing as he shouted at the driver.

"I know!" The driver said as he slammed on the brakes leaving a long line of rubber on the road with smoking tires as he shoved the car into reverse and began backing up. Cars were whizzing all around them swearing loudly.

"What are you? NUTS? You are going to kill us! And Benton said to follow them discreetly."

"Would you rather explain to Benton how we lost them?" The driver exclaimed as he continued accelerate backwards.

"Er...no. Keep going!" The other man responded. They lost count how many near misses they had and were sighing while crossing themselves once they were on the exit ramp.

Riccardo continued to accelerate, surprised by the car's quick response. "Did we lose them?" Crystal asked.

Riccardo looked in his mirrors seeing them several car lengths behind but gaining. "No I see them turning following us." The stretch of road they were on was vacant except for four large tractor trailers. He started to pass one and noticed the large logo on the side and smiled. "I have an idea. But you may not like it."

"I already don't like it. But I won't like what will happen if they catch us even more. Do it."

"All right, get out my phone. It is in the black bag behind my seat."

Crystal pulled the bag up into her lap and searched its contents. "Is this it?" She held out a rectangular electronic device with a touch screen and keypad.

"Yes. Turn it on and tap on the menu button, then tap code put in 6563321 truck access. Press the large speaker icon when it comes up."

"Okay." Crystal said as she keyed in the buttons in the proper sequence. "And done."

Riccardo checked the phones screen quickly and spoke even faster. "Convoy on A-1 this is Alpha-Diango. Verify."

The phone crackled for a second and a response was in a thick Italian accent. "Confirmed access. This is Convoy H-175 on A-1. Riccardo!? Is that you?"

"Savio? What are you doing here?"

"Training some of our men, you did tell me I needed to get out of the office more often," he said laughing.

"Not exactly what I meant, and you know it."

"Yes, I know it," he said still chuckling. "Where are you?"

"The small red car coming up on your left."

"That thing? You have got to be kidding. It is a scatola di pranzo!" Savio exclaimed.

"Wish I was. But in this case it may be to our advantage. Do you remember that old theoretical maneuver we once talked about?"

"Yes, the one you told us was too dangerous and never to try it?" Savio asked.

"That is the one. I have a problem. I have two men following us and I have to lose them."

"The black car coming up on us fast?"

"That is the one."

"Are you sure you want to do this? I mean ..." Savio's voice wavered.

"We don't have a choice Savio." Riccardo said with a bit of frustration in his voice.

"Say no more. Use the second trailer. I am in the first one. You know what to do and we will take care of the rest."

"Thanks." Riccardo said then turned to Crystal as he tapped the large mute button on his phone's screen. "Hang on. We are going to disappear." He accelerated past one of the large tractor trailers. Once they were past, he smiled as they approached the middle section of the second trailer and matched its speed. The third pulled out behind them as he carefully slid in underneath the second trailer's large section.

"Are you crazy?!?!" Crystal exclaimed seeing huge wheels spinning right in front of them. "This is insane! This is your plan?!"

"Well yes," Riccardo smiled. "I never thought I would be glad that this car is so small." The trailer behind them began accelerating until it was directly alongside. This blocked their pursuers line of sight and they sailed past the convoy without a second glance. After their pursers passed the first trailer, the trailer alongside Riccardo and Crystal accelerated until he was even with the first. Riccardo carefully eased the car out from underneath the second trailer and moved in behind the third.

Riccardo relaxed his grip on the wheel and tapped the phone. "Good work Savio. Keep this formation until the next turn off. Then we will drop back and you keep going. I hope you are not hauling anything dangerous."

"Well ..." Savio said sucking in a breath. "Class 5."

Riccardo went white. "Class 5? I thought we stopped doing that a month ago."

"This is the last load. It's why I am escorting it personally. And why did you *think* I asked if you were sure?" Savio chuckled. "I am just glad it worked."

"So am I. More than you know. Take care my friend and be sure to get this load to its destination safely." Riccardo said as they turned off down a side street, entering Zurich's city limits.

"We will. You know me." Savio said as the phone clicked off.

Crystal looked towards Riccardo. "So, what are they carrying?"

"I would rather not say," Riccardo sighed. "But at least this is the last load. Check the map I printed out earlier," he said as they sat at the first traffic light. "I think we take the next street to the right."

Back in the perusing car tempers were getting heated. "Where the heck are they? They can't be that far ahead of us." The man in the passenger seat exclaimed.

"I don't know. But we lost them. And *you* are telling Benton," the driver said.

"Hey it wasn't my fault. And you were driving!"

"Yes I am driving and you have to call, he is going to want a status report." The driver said while continuing to look around to make sure they didn't miss something.

"You have a point," the man said while dialing his phone. "Yes, umm we don't know where." The driver could over hear Benton's swearing from his seat as the phone was held out away from the other man's ear then moved back closer to talk. "Yes Sir, we did ...but then ...well ...they disappeared."

"You mean you lost them?!" Benton yelled. "How could you lose them?"

"I don't know. We were right on A1 not many were on the road at the time. We passed a few trucks, and they were gone."

"Trucks? Hmm ... assume they took the last turn off that you missed."

"Yes Sir." The man in the passenger seat said. "But we can't go back that far on this road. We will take the next one, but it will take a while to get back there. They will be long gone by then."

"You are lucky I considered this and have someone waiting inside Zurich. They will not get away. But don't think this lets you off of the hook. I will deal with you two later ... personally." Benton fumed as the line went dead.

The driver gulped. "I heard that. I think we had better find them first."

"You got that right ... for both our sakes." The other man said as they took the next exit and headed back towards Zurich.

Riccardo grumbled as they sat at another traffic light. "I forgot how much traffic–" Then stopped looking in his rear mirror. "No it can't be."

"What?" Crystal asked turning around.

"No, don't turn around." He said as he took a sudden turn to the right as soon as the light went green. A car behind them squealed its tires to follow them. "Dang it. I didn't give Benton enough credit." Riccardo gunned the engine and they took off on a side street with the car behind them in hot pursuit.

"I thought we lost them," Crystal said looking back.

"So did I. Obviously he had someone already watching for

us here. Hang on this is going to be tricky." He swerved into an intersection, did a 90 degree turn, and took off in another direction. Their pursuer was also a good driver, and they came right after them.

A light ahead of them turned red. "Hang on!" Riccardo shouted as he floored the accelerator diving into the traffic. Horns honked and tires made sounds of agony. They managed to get through before the intersection was hopelessly full of cars in various orientations. It would be some time before anyone else got through.

"There, I think we lost them." Riccardo said finally allowed himself to breathe. "That was too close."

"You're telling me!" Crystal said her face white.

Then they heard sirens. "Dang!" Riccardo muttered looking back. "The police are now after us. We can't let them pull us over. Benton has too many contacts, and we are wanted on Interpol at the moment." He dove into an alleyway, but the motorcycle policeman followed much to his dismay. Then as they popped out on the other side of the street, another police car gave chase.

"How many are there?" Crystal asked breathless as she saw another police car and heard more sirens in the distance.

"Too many," Riccardo grunted. "I don't know how I can avoid them all." He winced as another police car joined the chase.

They kept ducking and diving from one street to another. But every time they lost one car, there was another. Either the police or one of Benton's. "I can't keep this up for much longer. They are bound to catch us soon," Riccardo sighed. Then his eyes widened, and he made a quick turn heading west. "I have an idea."

"Will I like it?" Crystal said squeezing his knee.

"Probably not." Riccardo frowned.

"Great," Crystal sighed. "Should I ask?"

"No." Riccardo said as they approached a bridge. Large signs said "BRIDGE OUT" with yellow caution lights that flashed in front of them a second before they smashed through the thin wooden barricades.

"Is this your plan?" Crystal shrieked.

"Yes. But I know this bridge is not really out. They are doing minor maintenance. But no one will expect us to take this route. It should give us some breathing ... DANG IT!" He shouted as he saw the huge hole in the middle bridge and they were racing towards it at top speed. "They must have done that yesterday."

"Riccardo! Stop! We can't get around that!" Crystal exclaimed.

"I know!" But as he was about to slam on the brakes he hit the gas instead and pushed the peddle all the way to the floor.

"Riccardo what are you *doing*?!" Crystal shrieked as the sudden acceleration slammed her back into her seat. "STOP!"

There was a large pile of crushed asphalt with wooden boards laid over it to keep the rain off. "I have an idea! Hang on!"

"Wish you would quit saying that!" Crystal said with her heart in her throat.

Riccardo hit the huge mound of rock at high speed at just the right angle. They went up and sailed over the vast hole below landing *hard* on the other side. The shock system screamed with the sound of tortured metal and snapped. Tires exploded but Riccardo kept the accelerator pressed all the way down. A moment later the rims were carving deep gouges in the pavement. They made it off of the bridge and down the road on the other side when the engine could no longer take the strain and gave a final roar before several rods punctured the engine block. Acrid smoke spewed from under the hood and oil streaked the windshield.

Riccardo stood on the brake peddle trying to stop them but found that the hydraulics had also failed and what little was left were fading fast. It wasn't enough. He turned the wheel hard swerving to bleed off excess speed and avoid a lamppost. It almost worked. But the inertia was too great, and they hit the post sideways with a tremendous *crack*. Air bags popped, and they were encased in large smoking balloons.

They were pushing away the air bags when Riccardo's nose wrinkled at the smell of gas. "Crystal you okay?"

Crystal shook her head. "Yes. Seem to be. Still a little shaken but okay."

"Good we have to get out of here. I smell gas. This could blow any minute."

"I smell it too," Crystal said as she unbuckled her seat belt. Probably the only thing that kept her from broken bones. She pushed on the door which squealed with the sound of tortured metal as it ground open.

"Crystal, my seat belt won't unlock." Riccardo said as he continued to pull at the restraint. The smell of gas wafting throughout the car was getting stronger. They knew it could erupt into a fireball any second. "Crystal! Go! Please!"

"I won't leave you!" Crystal shrieked tears running down her cheeks.

"You must go ... *now!* My spirit couldn't bear it if you were to come to harm. *Please.*"

Crystal shook her head and pulled at the belt. Silently cursing that the airlines didn't allow her to keep her pocket knife. "No! I won't leave you!"

"*Please!*" Riccardo took her hands and looked deep into her eyes.

She pulled at the belt several more times, took a deep breath, kissed him quickly, got out, and ran. She turned around in time to see the car explode in a huge ball of flame. "Riccardo!" She cried with her hand outstretched. With tears running down her cheeks and looking down as she shook all over, she didn't notice a man coming up from behind. The crunch of broken glass underfoot snapped her back to reality and turned around to see a big man placing a cloth on her face. She smelled something chemical, and all went black.

29

Crystal fought against the inky blackness that had consumed her consciousness. Images of the car exploding flooded her mind. She forced them back. The blackness relented and her senses started to return. The first was a blinding headache. "Ow!" she thought. Then feeling returned to her hands ...feet ...legs ...arms ...as they inched back to life. Her nose wrinkled at the strong smell of mold and dampness. She could now feel the restraints around her chest, arms, and legs.

"She is starting to come around," a distant voice said.

She felt herself sitting upright, in a chair she thought. Crystal pulled her head up and fought to open her eyes. The blinding light forced them to close almost as quick. "Ugh." The groan came out louder than she intended. She forced her eyes open again, and the pain was less this time. Someone was standing in front of her. A man, but it was hard to tell at this point. She blinked again and again. Finally, the form resolved into a tall man wearing a black turtleneck with dark pants.

The man's muscles bulged as he folded his arms and stared at Crystal. "Welcome back to the land of the living," he said in a thick Italian accent.

Crystal never thought she would be tired of Italian accents

but at this moment, she changed her mind. "Am I? I'm not sure yet," she groaned. Her head thumped but everything else felt okay. Slow, distant, but intact. Her head started to clear, and she thought it must have been whatever they used to knock her out. She looked around and couldn't see very far outside the cone of light shining down overhead. It was the only light in the room and directed to make sure everything, except her, to remain dark. She could see a table just inside the light's influence with her purse and its contents laid out on the table.

"Yes you are," the man said. "Now where is it?" he growled.

Crystal blinked. "Where is what?" She wiggled in her seat, fighting against the ropes that held her.

"You know very well what I mean. Riccardo didn't have it, so you must." The man stood looking very irritated.

"I don't know what you mean." Crystal said in the strongest voice she could muster. "They must want the keycard," she thought. Riccardo would have died for nothing if they were to get it and she was not about to let them win.

The man sprang forward placing both hands on either arm of the chair coming within inches of her face and shouted. "Don't play games with me! We have no patience for this. You have caused us enough grief. Now either tell me now, or we will use other ... means."

Crystal winced and thought this guy ate far too much garlic. Then wiggled again in her seat and this time she felt it. Something tucked inside her bra.

"Don't bother trying to get free," the man sneered. "Those ropes are far too tight," he said backing away. "Again I will ask you. Where is it? We know you have a special electronic keycard in your possession. Where is it? This is the last time I will ask."

Crystal looked towards the table and her eyes widened. "Ohh! It's here is it?" The man went over inspecting the table and its contents.

"Er no ... it ... I mean I don't ... " she trailed off.

"Don't bother, your body language has told me all I need to know." He said reaching for the purse itself and feeling it all over. Then separated the cover from the rest of the purse he produced an encoded plastic card with the Zero emblem clearly visible on it. "Here it is!"

"Give it to me!" A voice shouted from the darkness. Crystal immediately recognized the voice as Benton's. So he was here in person. The Crystal heard heavy footsteps, saw a hand enter the lighted area, and the card was dropped into it. "Finally!" Benton exclaimed as the card shook in his hand. "It's mine. After all this time, it's *mine.*" Benton said as Crystal heard him walk away. Then the sound of a door being unlocked came from dark recesses of the room, light poured in as it opened. She could see several men as dark outlines against the doorway.

"What shall we do with her?" A man in the said as he jerked a thumb in Crystal's direction. She could tell by his voice it was the man in the black turtleneck.

"Leave her," Benton said. "If something goes wrong, we will need her. But if not the rats will take care of her ... eventually." Benton sneered and Crystal heard the door slam behind them. Then the clink of several deadbolts as the door was sealed.

Crystal yanked at her restrains. The man had been right, they were too tight. But she continued to try anyway. Over and over again she yanked and wiggled trying to get free.

Now that it was quiet, she could make out the sound of dripping water in the distance and figured she must be in a basement ... somewhere. But that also meant no one was likely to find her, let alone hear her cries for help. She sighed wondering what to do.

Just as she had resigned herself to her fate, she heard the door's bolts click and slide back. "Oh no, they are coming back?" She wondered while looking towards the door. A moment later it opened showing only white light in a rectangular vertical frame in the distance. She saw two figures stand in its frame, talking in Italian for a moment, then entered closing the door behind them.

Crystal sat wondering what they were going to do to her. Seconds dragged by, feeling like hours. Then one man came into range of the overhead light with a finger by his nose. "Riccardo!" she squeaked as quietly as she could

"La Mia Signora. I told you I wouldn't leave you." He said with a smile and began untying her.

"But but but you're dead! The car ... "

"Well I can assure you I am not. Yes the car did explode, but I forgot I had a knife in my pocket and managed to cut the belt and get out right before. The explosion threw me clear, and I was knocked unconscious for a while but alive."

"How did you find me?"

"I still have a couple of people in Benton's organization that owed me a few favors. I used them all up to find out where you were. I am sorry I couldn't be here sooner but I knew he would leave you once he had the card. Being alone, I couldn't take them all on by myself. Certainly not without them harming you, which I couldn't have. I am glad you are all right. It is all that matters."

"But what about the key?"

"It doesn't matter now. I know we won't get it back from Benton without some sort of full scale assault, and that is not something I am about to do. It is not worth it," Riccardo said shaking his head.

"Oh Riccardo!" Crystal said wrapping her arms around him. He responded holding her tight.

"La Mia Signora. There is time for that later. I need to finish untying you and we have to get out of here. My agreement is only for fifteen minutes. After that we will be reported and chased."

"Where are we?" Crystal said standing as Riccardo loosened the last of the ropes and let them fall to the ground.

"In the basement of one of Benton's warehouses. I am not sure what he uses this one for, and to be honest, I don't want to." He said putting everything on the table back into her purse then grabbed her hand squeezing. "Let's go," he said as they ran for the door.

The air outside the building was damp and dreary from the recent rains. They both sighed slowing their pace with the feeling they had avoided detection and were away from that terrible place.

"Hold it right there," a voice called out. They froze in place, not daring to breathe. A moment later a large bruit of a man came into the light waving his shiny gun equipped with a silencer.

Riccardo swore under his breath has he held up his hands and gestured for Crystal to do the same. "I don't know him, and I am sure he can't be bribed as is with most of Benton's men," Riccardo whispered. "I will tackle him once he gets closer and you run. I will be along in a minute. If we do it fast, he won't have time to respond."

"I won't leave you here." Crystal held up her hands as the man continued to approach.

"Don't worry I will be right behind you," Riccardo whispered.

Crystal's eyes flashed, and she smiled. "I have a better idea."

"Like what?"

"You'll see." She smiled and winked as she slipped her hand into her purse.

"You two stop talking." The large man sneered. "Turn around and walk back the way you came."

"Right now?" Crystal asked.

"Yes right now. Wait! Take your hand out of that bag!" He pointed to Crystal's purse. "Slowly!"

Crystal removed her hand while still concealing a little cylinder.

"Now hand me that bag." He took Crystal's purse in his other hand. "Thought you would surprise me with your gun did you?" He chuckled, then peered inside.

"Don't you know it's not polite to look in a ladies purse?" Crystal shouted. As the man looked up, a fine mist sprayed from the cylinder in her hand and made direct contact with his face.

His eyes widened, and he raised his gun. "Why you ... " But never finished the sentence. He stood there paralyzed in mid-step.

"What did you do?" Riccardo blinked.

"Hit him with some pepper spray," Crystal said taking her purse back from the goon's grip.

"I have never seen pepper spray do that!" Riccardo exclaimed. "Where did you get it?"

"A friend gave it to me before I left for Italy."

"Oh really? And am I going to meet this friend?" Riccardo said with a smile.

"May be. But shall we get out of here? I don't know how long that will hold him."

"Of course," Riccardo said as he grabbed her hand and they bolted for the car he had waiting for them.

A few moments later Crystal and Riccardo were sitting in a newly rented large blue sports car some distance from the warehouse as he started the engine. "How did you manage to get this so fast? Didn't the situation with Interpol give a problem?" Crystal wondered aloud.

"My contact came through and proved the info was fraudulent so they called off the alert," Riccardo said.

"Oh good, then we aren't wanted fugitives anymore."

"Officially no, but it may take a little time for it to filter down to every level. We are lucky, where I rented this, it already had." Riccardo said then sat back and sighed.

"What is it?"

"I wish we didn't lose the card. I know that we can't get it now, it is certainly not worth the risk. But Benton should not have Terrance's discovery whatever it is."

"Well ... " Crystal grinned as she reached into her blouse and a moment later produced a plastic card. "He won't without this."

"La Mia Signora! What? How?" Riccardo said as he took the card from Crystal's fingers and examined it.

"Well you know when I told you that we did the advertising campaign for Zero?"

Riccardo nodded.

"During their first week of operation they gave out business cards that looked a lot like their keycards. Not many were given out because people were getting confused. Zero had too many complaints from its staff with people trying to use the business cards as keycards." Crystal pointed to the card in Riccardo's grasp. "This card is real. Benton has one of the business cards that Zero gave me months ago."

"Remind me never to cross you." Riccardo said as he put the card in his pocket.

"Are you sure? I might let you, and who knows, you might like it." Crystal winked.

Riccardo laughed. "Perhaps I will take you up on that after all. Okay, next stop Zero Stor!" He said as they left the parking lot and headed east towards a large tower with ZS clearly labeled on its side.

30

Crystal and Riccardo walked into Zero's huge reception area. The marble floor at the entry soon gave way into high quality carpeting just past reception heading towards offices or rooms. A large sign in black with gold lettering high above was clearly embellished with their core ideals for all to see:

Zero Theft

Zero Hassle

Zero Problems

As they approached the counter, the receptionist greeted them in German accented English. "Welcome to Zero. How may I help you today?"

Riccardo showed the keycard to her. "We have an account and would like to access it please."

"Certainly sir. Will you need assistance or will you prefer to do everything yourselves?"

Riccardo looked towards Crystal and she nodded. "I think we can handle it, thank you."

"Very well. Examination room 4 is currently available. It is down the hall and third door on the right," the receptionist said pointing.

"Thank you." Riccardo took Crystal's hand, they walked down the hall. A moment later they were inside a large conference room. A sizable wooden table with an impressive Z marble insert sat in the center and several black leather office chairs surrounding it. In the back, a computer console with some sort of large sliding door next do it. "I assume you know how this works?" He looked towards Crystal.

"Yes. Put the keycard in the slot on the console, Z side up and it should acknowledge the card, then give us an options screen." Crystal said walked over and pointed to a small slot just below the screen with a big arrow pointing towards it.

"Sounds simple enough." Riccardo said, but as he was about to insert the card, the intercom speaker above them came to life.

"Security to Examination Room 2. Security to Examination Room 2." It crackled as the microphone turned off.

Crystal blinked. "Is that us?"

"No we are in room 4. But room 2 must be nearby. I am going to take a look." Riccardo said as he walked to the other side of the room. "I think I hear shouting." He opened the door a crack. The muffled voices were now clear.

"You are making a mistake!" Benton whaled. "Check it again!"

"Sir, I have checked four times. That card does not apply to any account here. I am sorry." A man in a well tailored suit said as several other large men appeared both wearing weapons. "Now these men will escort you off of the premises."

"You are lying! You want to keep it for yourself!" Benton's exasperated voice faltered slightly under the strain.

The man shook his head. "Sir, we have no idea what is in any account. That is how we do business. Our system does not even store a name or any identifiable information other than the account number which is triple encoded on a pass card. Without a fully working pass card nothing can be retrieved. We cannot override the system, nor can we search for something in particular as I already told you. Now please leave or we will be forced to make your withdrawal very unpleasant. Do I make myself clear?"

"Yes," Benton snarled. "Quite clear." His words stressed through gritted teeth. "But know this . . . I am not done here. I shall be back."

"No, you won't. We do not take threats here very well. You shall not be allowed on these premises now or ever. Now go. This is the last time I will say it."

"You just made an enemy." Benton said through pursed lips. "And I am going." As he turned to leave, Riccardo carefully closed the door and flipped the lock. While he was sure that the manager could open the door, it would keep Benton from peeking in as he walked by.

"Let's see what our card will do." Riccardo said after he walked back across the room and inserted the key into the slot. The console's screen lit up and listed several language options. He selected English. A moment later the screen lit up with "Please enter passcode."

"Passcode?" Crystal blinked. "Did the Professor tell you anything?"

"Nothing about a password or code. Although he did mail me that odd message along with the card. I never did understand what he meant. But now I think I do. It must be the password."

"Yes it has to be. What did he say again?"

"Hmm let me think," Riccardo said looking distant. "Zero Has it, Please take care of it 453439524210420471RetroEpsilon."

"Are you sure? We only have three chances to try. If we

enter wrong code three times, the card is locked, and the stored contents are destroyed with a thermite charge built into all storage boxes."

"Wow and I thought I took security seriously. Yes I am certain, I will never forget that letter. It was as you say, 'burned into my memory'," Riccardo said as he punched in the numbers on the keypad.

A moment later the screen read "Incorrect passcode. You have two chances remaining before emergency procedures are activated."

"Should have known Terrance would not make it that simple," Riccardo sighed. "Hmm Reto ... that means backwards in Latin. Perhaps it means the numbers must be entered in reverse."

"Worth a try." Crystal shrugged as Riccardo began entering the long numeral string.

But a moment later, "Incorrect passcode. You have one chance remaining before emergency procedures are activated." flashed on the screen.

"Hmm Terrance certainly made this a puzzle. I know Epsilon is Greek but not sure how that help us here," Riccardo sighed.

Crystal thought for a moment. "Isn't Epsilon a letter in the Greek alphabet? I don't know how we can ... " She trailed off then her eyes grew wide. "Oh wait, unicode!"

Riccardo looked at her as his eyebrows rose. "Unicode?"

"Yes Unicode. It allows for characters not normally on a keyboard to be used. We often need to for our advertising clients. So it may mean to enter the Epsilon last via Unicode. Let me think ... that should be U+0395. And this console has a full keyboard. Try it. Numbers in reverse, then add the Unicode Epsilon with U+0395 on the number pad at the end."

"Okay," Riccardo said his fingers poised over the keyboard, "here goes." He began keying in the long number sequence then added the Epsilon character as Crystal described.

A moment later they were greeted with "Passcode accepted. Would you like to retrieve your account now?" Riccardo pressed "Yes" and the screen flashed "Thank you. Please stand by." A few moments later the four-foot square door slid up and a robotic arm placed a three-foot box on the platform under it. The arm retracted, and the door closed.

The box was white except for the large black Z emblem on the top. Riccardo tentatively felt its weight, while heavy it was not extreme and placed it on the table. Upon opening the overlapping plastic cover flaps they found a cardboard shipping box almost as large. The second box contained large but thin stone tablet, a notebook and a small electronic device of some sort. All were carefully packed.

"What is this?" Crystal asked picking up the small device. It was almost six inches long but very thin, lightweight, and fit well in her hand.

"It is a small holographic video recorder he was working on. I know Terrance often made notes with it as well." Riccardo said as he looked at the device then frowned as the screen came on. "There is only one file here, and it had to be recorded right after I met with him." He pushed play and light flashed around the room slowly resolving above the table into the image of Professor Terrance Croorlheart looking very haggard as though he had not slept in weeks. He spoke in heavy, rough, Italian voice.

"My friend, if you are seeing this I have failed to bring to the world the greatest discovery mankind has ever seen. It has the potential to rewrite everything and change the course of human endeavors. I had hoped to show you this in person and have you help me, but due to people that want this discovery for selfish reasons I found myself needing to take flight. I cannot get into the details of my discovery here as I do not have time. Nor can I trust this location is secure. I suspect I am being watched. I have been watched for weeks. Everywhere I go, they are there. I can't seem to lose them. His reach is too great. I only hope you can do better than I."

"Wow." Crystal said louder than she intended and Ricardo quickly put a finger to his lips for silence.

"I am sending my notes, this recording and the center item that started all of this to Zero," the Professor continued. "It should be secure there until you can retrieve it. I will get the key to you somehow. Please take good care of this. I know you will. I am only sorry I couldn't show and explain it to you in person. God Speed my friend." The hologram dissolved into random light beams before disappearing entirely.

Crystal picked up the thick notebook with its well-used cover and carefully leafed through its pages. Many of the pages had seen heavy use. "It's all in Italian." She said handing the book over to Riccardo.

"I am not surprised," he said as he began to read. "It would seem, he found this old tablet and began its translation. At first he thought it was just another story of Atlantis. But then he realized it was more. Much more. It was an accurate historical account of the City of Atlantis."

"You mean the city actually existed?" Crystal blinked.

"Yes. According to this, it was far too detailed and accurate to be a simple story. And he found other evidence."

"I can see why he wanted to keep this secret, it's so amazing to be unbelievable. He actually found proof Atlantis existed? But what was this about a power source and something that he didn't want to fall into the wrong hands?" Crystal wondered aloud.

"I don't know." Riccardo he sat in one of the well-padded chairs surrounding the conference table. "Ah I think I found it." He thumbed through the notebook's pages. "Atlantis was an advanced group of humans. While that is nothing new, this part is: they were from another world. A parallel Earth or another dimension. From what Terrance could translate, their Earth did not have the same barbaric period that we did in our early history. A race of humans that learned to work together as a planet and live in peace.

"The problem was, at some point their world started dying. But they never understood why. Their world increased in volcanic activity, tremors, and earthquakes. They had tried many methods to save their planet but nothing worked. In the end most of their population had died. However, they were not about to give up. In a last ditch effort they started a new project and devoted all their resources to it. 'The Dimensional Door' they called it. And managed to create a rip in space and this allowed them to come to our Earth. They thought the world was uninhabited, moved across, and built Atlantis. However, after a time they found the humans here on another content. They tried to set up trade with them, but the barbaric, primitive humans were either living in fear of them or thinking of them as gods.

"They knew that sooner or later the inhabitant of this world would rally against them out of fear, so they built a backup city in secret and called it Sitnalta. But in time they came to doubt the wisdom of this and wondered if they had the right to live on a world when they were not from it. Soon after Sitnalta was completed, Atlantis was attacked. While they did defend themselves with ease using their technology, it was at great cost to the attacking humans. Some did flee, but most refused and fought to the death which greatly surprised the inhabitants of Atlantis.

"Fearing that only more life would be lost–something intolerable to them–or worse: the development of this world changed because they were seen as gods and worshiped. The people of Atlantis decided to try to find another world, one that was uninhabited and destroy their city.

"One man was left behind to activate the destruct and sink the great city. And while he was given orders to destroy Sitnalta as well, he did not. Instead, he hid it and left clues for it to be found in the future when mankind was old enough. A gift to them even if it would take a vast amount of time before they could claim it."

"Incredible." Crystal said as she sat in one of the chairs. "So Atlantis existed, and its inhabitants were from a parallel universe that came here. They left, destroyed Atlantis but the backup city Sitnalta was left behind hidden for us to claim at some point? No wonder the professor didn't want Benton to get his hands on this."

"Indeed. Apparently this is the key to the city." Riccardo pointed to the piece of stone resting inside the cardboard box.

"Do we know where the city is?" Crystal said unable to curb the excitement in her voice.

"Not exactly. It seems he was not finished with the translation. He had a rough idea but not an exact location. He knew it was somewhere in South America."

"Has to be somewhere in the Amazon then, it would have been found otherwise," Crystal said thinking of the dense jungle. "How do we find it? The Amazon is a big place."

Riccardo smiled. "Well I finish the translation and we see where it takes us."

"You can read that? It looks like Greek to me." She pointed to the stone tablet.

"Yes, it is actually. Ancient Greek to be exact." He said straight-faced while looking at the tablet. "I have studied Ancient Greek. This appears to be an unusual dialect of it, but I should be able to figure it out."

"Wow, I am impressed. I always thought it was a hard language."

"It's not that bad, really. I know several other languages besides English, Spanish, Portuguese, and Italia."

"Okay, you just impressed me more. So Mr. Linguistic, what does this say?"

Riccardo looked at Crystal with a blank look. "Mr. Linguistic?" His eyebrows met, then after a few moments, laughed. "Ohh ... very funny. Well as I said this is a different form of Ancient Greek and I should be able to translate it. But let's do that back at the hotel. I think we have spent enough time here."

"I agree." Crystal said as she placed the holographic recorder back in the Professor's cardboard box. "I think we should return the Zero box back to storage."

Riccardo nodded. "Good idea. The account might be useful." Crystal closed the flaps on the black box, placed it on the platform and pressed the return key on the console. The door slide open and the robotic arm gripped the box with the door sliding closed right after it. She grabbed the keycard as the console ejected it with a confirmation message.

By now Riccardo had placed everything into the Professor's box then walked over to the door, opened it gesturing towards the doorway. "Shall we, La Mia Signora?"

"We shall." She looped her arm through his as they left Zero together.

31

Crystal and Riccardo sat at the table in a hotel examining the Professor's tablet. He had registered them both with fictitious names, and another hotel with their actual names several hours distance, for when Benton came looking for them. Riccardo was sure Benton had found Crystal gone by now and could only imagine his rage.

"I am surprised the Professor didn't finish the translation." Crystal said as she watched Riccardo work, then gazed out the window to see the sun slip below the horizon.

"Terrance had concerns about the security of what he had found. He was also very short on time. Combine the two and he didn't finish even though he wanted to very badly. And I think I have found out why Benton is perusing us."

"Oh?" Crystal blinked.

"Yes, after reviewing the notebook a bit more, I found part of the Terrance's research was funded by Benton."

"What?!" Crystal exclaimed. "Why would Benton fund research? Doesn't sound like him. Or the more important question: Why would the Professor ask him and not you?" She said sitting down in the other padded chair.

"It would seem he didn't want to come to me since I had helped him on another project. Benton approached to him offering, and at the time, Terrance thought was a good idea. He didn't know Benton was actually Benito Giordano. He only found out later, and by then Benton had learned too much to let him go. One item to our advantage ... Benton does not know what the discovery actually is. Terrance couldn't hide his enthusiasm so he told Benton it was a new incredible source of power. While true, if not exact."

"That is definitely a benefit." Crystal said as Riccardo continued to study the tablet, switching between it and his laptop every few minutes. "Any luck in finding out where Sitnalta is located?"

"Yes. Translating is slow. As I said it is an unusual form of Ancient Greek. But with Terrance's notes I am making progress. It is obviously on South America as the descriptions fit. Even after thousands of years. But this is going to take a while." He said while gazing at the tablet, then switched back to his computer's screen.

Crystal's stomach knotted, and she looked at the clock, it was well past dinner time. "Hungry?" she asked.

"Very much so," Riccardo said looking up. "But I didn't realize it until now." He chuckled gazing back at his screen.

"I will go get us something. I saw a buffet laid out just inside the dinning room as we came up here." Crystal said as she shouldered her purse and walked towards the door.

"Hmmm?" Riccardo looked up from his screen. "Yes thank you." He said as Crystal closed the door behind her.

Crystal walked to the elevator and went back down to the ground floor. She let her nose guide her and a few moments later she was looking at the large assortment of items on the restaurant's buffet. It was an impressive layout, even with most of the labels in German.

"Can I help you?" One of the hotel staff asked in German

accented English. He noticed her look around then bite her lip.

"Oh, no thank you. I'm just getting a few items to take up to my room." Crystal grabbed a couple of plates and placed them on one of the wooden trays sitting in a pile alongside.

"What is your room number please?"

"24, is there a problem?"

"No problem at all." The man smiled. "I wanted to make sure you were staying here. Dinner is free to current guests. Please take whatever you like and let me know if I can be of assistance."

"Of course, and thank you."

"You are welcome. Enjoy your stay." The man turned and walked off, attending to others in the restaurant.

Crystal placed several items on the plates and headed back up to her room where she found Riccardo looking even more intense than when she left. "Dinner is served," she said with a smile placing a plate of food in front of him, which until that moment, had not noticed her return.

"Oh thank you." The wonderful aromas wafted up to his nose forcing him to look down. "Zopf, rosti, and nusstorte, looks great." He said cutting a piece of zopf and popping it into his mouth. "And of good quality too."

"I am glad you like it, to be honest I have no idea what all it is. The labels were in German," Crystal said sitting down. "Although I did identify one item," she said producing a bowl of melted cheese with several dipping forks. "Fondue is the same in any language." She smiled sampling some fondue and sat down in one of the well padded chairs next to Riccardo.

"Ah, you see zopf is a type of Swiss bread, but I think you figured that out. Bread is pretty universal." Riccardo smiled.

"Rosti is something like your hash browns I believe you call them. And nusstorte is a very delicious nut cake."

"It does sound delicious. Glad I made good choices, even if blind. I also got some rubeli kuchen, whatever that is. It smelled good though."

"That is a Swiss carrot cake," Riccardo smiled.

"Well no wonder I liked the smell. I love carrot cake!" She said dipping some zopf into the fondue. "Any luck on where in South America Sitnalta is?"

"Yes I have. It is in the Guiana Highlands." Riccardo said while munching on some rosti.

"What makes you so sure? And where is the Guiana Highlands?"

"Well, this tablet mentions a great range of animals and the Guiana Highlands are the only place in the world with that kind of bio diversity. Some specimens only exist there. And in fact no one knows why or how it came to have such a range of biological life. As to where it is, that varies. It covers several countries in the northern section of South America. However, most of it is in Venezuela. But one part has me rather confused."

"Do you think they might have brought species from their Earth?" Crystal said as she sat closer dipping another piece of zopf into the fondue. "And what has you confused?"

"Yes it makes sense that they would try to save what they could. Probably before they realized humans were on this planet as well. But it says here that we need to find 'water from heaven then look away and seek between to the pillars letting the setting sun guide you'."

"Sounds like a riddle."

"Yes could be. Or that people didn't have GPS back then, and they had to use well-known identifying markers. But what they thought was well-known then is totally different today." Riccardo said as he finished the last of the Rosti and started on the nut cake.

"Isn't Angel Falls in Venezuela?"

"Yes it is. But I am sure they didn't use that name back in Atlantis' day."

"I am sure, but is it in the Guiana Highlands area you mentioned?"

"Yes, it is near the front edge actually," Riccardo said nodding. "But I am not sure what you are getting at?"

"Well, even though we are certain they didn't call it Angel Falls back then, it is still the tallest water falls in the world. If someone stands at its base and looks up, it would look as though water is falling from heaven," Crystal said smiling.

Riccardo had a blank look for a moment then his eyes widened. "You're right! Why didn't I think of that? And Angel falls is far older than Atlantis, they would have seen it very similar to today."

"Exactly," Crystal said sitting back in the chair having finished her dinner.

Riccardo worked on his computer for a few moments then smiled. "I found an available flight to Venezuela tomorrow and reserved a seat."

"And what about me?"

Riccardo shook his head. "La Mia Signora, I have already endangered you far too much. Venezuela is not exactly the most stable country in the world, and while it is decent at the moment, it is not a place for tourists."

"Riccardo Marino! If *you* think you are going to leave me behind now, you have another thing coming." She took his hands in hers. "We are in this together, I wouldn't leave you behind and there is no way you are going to leave me behind either. Do you hate me that much?"

Riccardo blinked. "Where did *that* come from?" he asked himself. "Hate you? I don't hate you! I couldn't hate you if I wanted to!"

"Well you were going to leave me behind."

"But–"

"No buts," she said smiling. "You have often said you couldn't bear it if I were to come to harm. How do you think I would feel if you were hurt or killed, and I had no idea? To go through the rest of my life wondering what happened to you? I couldn't bear that either."

"All right ...all right ...all *right*. I relent. I think you say 'uncle' or something?"

Crystal laughed. "Yes that is an old expression to give in or relent."

"Well I do." The computer beeped, and he pointed at the screen. "There two seats on a flight to Venezuela for tomorrow afternoon. We had better go shopping again in the morning, it is not exactly the easiest of trips to get there. A long boat ride, followed by an even longer hike. We will need appropriate clothes and supplies. Are you sure you want to do this?"

Crystal rolled her eyes. "I thought we settled that?"

"All right ...alllll right. Can't blame me for trying." Riccardo held up his hands.

"Nope I can't." She said pulling him closer, and kissed his wonderful lips. "But I am glad you tried. Now let's get some rest, from what you said it sounds like we will need it."

"That we will." Riccardo said shutting off the computer and climbing into the queen-sized bed. Crystal followed silently wishing their clothes did not incinerate with the car, but they would fix that problem in the morning. She flipped off the light, squeezed Riccardo, and he squeezed back as they drifted off to sleep.

32

Benton paced the floor in the damp basement that only a few hours ago held his prize. Circling the chair again and again with the single light shining down from above. "How could you let her escape? How?!" He fumed

"I don't know Sir ... she must have–" One man started to say.

"SLIENCE!" Benton shouted. "The fault is yours and yours alone. I told you to watch her!"

"Sir ... you told me to–"

"SLIENCE! Do not contradict me!" Benton said as he leapt towards the man jabbing his finger in his face. "You know the price of failure." He turned away and took a step. The man sighed with relief then Benton waved his hand and another man stepped forward and put a sliced pistol in the other man's back. His eyes went wide just before three soft *thuds* were heard and the target of Benton's rage fell over twitching slightly but very ... dead.

Benton didn't turn. He continued to face the blackness of the room beyond the light. Then spoke over his shoulder. "Now for the rest of you, if you don't want to end up like him, find that woman! Riccardo must have been behind it! I want them found and I want it done yesterday. Use all of our resources, they must be in Zurich somewhere. Watch all flights out of the city. I don't want a flea leaving this city we don't know about. Do you understand?"

They all nodded and said "Yes Sir," in unison then began to leave.

"Good, then you may live to see another day." Benton said as he pulled a phone from his pocket and began dialing. "Yes it is I. I know I don't normally call myself but in this case I am not trusting this to anyone else. I want someone found, they are somewhere here in Zurich, a couple. I need them found as soon as possible. Yes I know it will be expensive, but I don't care. Use everyone, I want them found." Benton resumed pacing as he left the dark room. A man in a well tailored suit appeared near the door. But as he parted his lips to speak Benton made a gesture for silence. "Killed? No ... not yet. Only found and followed. I don't care if this sounds like me or not, do as I say or I will have someone visit you later. Understood? Good." The phone clicked off, and he turned to the suited man in front of him. "What is it Fedele?"

"Sir are you certain this location is compromised?" Fedele asked.

Benton gestured towards the stairs leading up to the ground floor of the warehouse and began to climb them. "Yes. While I doubt Riccardo will report us at the moment, he will do so in the near future."

"Are you sure? You know our financial status is ... quite precarious at the moment and it will be expensive to relocate." He said as they walked along large crates containing all manner of illicit contents. They passed three that held drugs, guns, and the last one had black market electronic equipment.

"I know. However, it would be even worse to have all of

this found by the Swiss Police. At least if we move we can still make use of it." Benton sighed as he looked among the various crates.

"Well we could have 'accident' and claim the insurance . . . " Fedele said letting his words to hang in the air.

"Yes, we could. But wouldn't we get more from moving and selling the inventory?"

Fedele did a few quick calculations in his head that would have taken others an hour. His ability with figures left little doubt why Benton had him in charge of the financial affairs. And his loyalty was unquestionable, not to mention about the only man Benton trusted fully. After a minute Fedele nodded. "You are right Sir, it would result in more profit. But the time factor is what has me concerned, an insurance claim would be quicker."

"Normally I would agree with you. But we lost a location only nine months ago. Granted we couldn't have prevented it, but the insurance company won't see it that way." Benton said as they walked past some pallets containing several large plasma televisions strapped together and wrapped in protective padding.

"Yes I see your point. I will begin moving preparations. Shall I prioritize selling or moving?"

"Selling. I think we have some time yet. Get it moved as soon as you can, but not at a loss. If it's going to be a loss, ship it instead. Hopefully this will lower the costs."

Fedele did more calculations the smiled. "You are correct Sir. It will, but there is one other aspect."

Benton stopped and turned to face him then cocked an eyebrow. "Which is?"

"Our liquid resources are low enough at the moment that there is a risk of foreclosure."

"No one is going to foreclose on US!" Benton shouted. "They would not dare!"

Fedele sighed then continued. "Are you forgetting that some people we owe would also very much like to see us out of business and will take any advantage they can get?"

Benton's face went cold, and he took a step back. It was only to be a very short loan, but the conditions did allow them to demand up to three quarters before the due date if there was a real reason for doing so. Normally it would not be a problem, but now ... "All right Fedele, liquidate it as fast as possible and put priority to pay back the intimidate debts. I don't want this hovering over us. Do we have enough to cover?"

Fedele looked towards the ceiling in deep thought. "Yes I think so. But after the recent losses, it's going to be close."

"Do it. And keep me informed."

"Yes, of course. I always do." He said turning to leave as another man ran towards them.

"I think we have a lead Sir! One of our informants says he has seen the woman."

"Wonderful!" Benton said making a grasping motion that turned into a hard fist. "It will yet me mine. Where are they?"

"Umm ... Sir ... he wouldn't say. He wants two million euro before he will tell us."

"What! How *dare* he! Have you explained what will happen to him if he *doesn't* tell us?"

"Yes Sir, but he doesn't seem to think we can at the moment for some reason."

"Doesn't think we can? I do not make threats, I make promises. Does he think he is dealing with a stolto?" Benton turned toward Fedele. "Can we afford to pay him for say an hour? Or at least make him think we did?"

Fedele shook his head. "Pay no, but yes I think I can fake it for that long."

Benton smiled and turned back "Tell him we will pay. Once he is confident and tells us the information, have him ... dealt with."

"Yes Sir."

"Oh and make sure he is taken care of ... very ... slowly. Try to hold me for random will he!" After the other man ran off Benton turned again back to Fedele. "How did anyone else find out about our situation?"

"I do not know. But it could be that when we took out that one loan, it was assumed. I told you that might happen."

Benton looked towards the ground. "Yes I know, but I thought we would have recovered that by now, it was only meant to be a one-week loan if that."

"I know Sir but after the loss of the other location we also lost the inventory purchased using that loan. And you told me not to increase the insurance. It did not come close to the real value."

Benton sighed. "I know. I thought it would be a waste, and the assets would have been moved in less than a week."

"We will pull through, Sir. We always do," Fedele smiled.

"Yes we will. And I will have my prize." Benton straightened as his eyes narrowed. "Liquidate this as soon as you can, but try not to lose too much. If you can make extra, do so. But the priority is paying back that loan."

"Yes, Sir. I will get right on it." Fedele said as he turned walking away to take a quick inventory before going back to his makeshift office in the corner of the warehouse.

33

Crystal emerged from the plane into the hot sticky hair that enveloped her in a long wet blanket. The air stank of jet fuel and almost choked her with the humidity. Standing on the tarmac, she could feel the heat emanating from it even through her shoes. She sighed and muttered "Welcome to Venezuela."

"What was that?" Riccardo turned to her.

"Nothing, I was noticing the weather."

"It is rather warm. I suspected it would be as being the middle of the summer." He smiled and took her hand. "Let's get through the baggage claim and then charter a flight."

Crystal's eyes widened. "Another one? I thought we were there?"

"The country yes. But we need to hire a small plane that will get us closer to Angel Falls. Then a boat trip for an hour or so. Then it is likely we will have to go the rest of the way on foot." Riccardo saw her grimace. "Well, you were the one that wanted to come."

Crystal snorted. "Don't remind me. This is going to ruin my hair."

"La Mia Signora, you have never looked more beautiful," Riccardo smiled.

Crystal blushed and kissed him softly as they waited near the luggage conveyer. Baggage bounced along as it ran, shuttered and then bounced again. They both winced at the rough treatment the various items received, praying the electronic equipment they had packed survived the trip. While they both held bags, some items didn't fit and required being sent to the plane's cargo hold.

"There they are." Crystal said with a sigh, pointing to two neon green heavy-duty travel backpacks appeared through the curtain. Since all the rest appeared to be black, blue, or beige she was fairly certain these were theirs.

"Yes, these are ours." Riccardo said upon grabbing both bags and checking the tags. He produced his key and unlocked them both checking the contents. "And still intact," he said with a smile, "okay let's see if we can find a guide that will take us to the base of Angel Falls. I heard the best local tour company is on the other side of this airport."

A few moments later Riccardo fought not to strangle the man behind the desk. "What do you mean you don't have anyone for four days?! I called ahead and was assured that a guide would be available."

"I am sorry senor, we only have two guides that will do what you want. And they are both out giving other tours and won't be back for at least four days. Most times it is not a problem." The clerk behind the counter sighed. "I wish I could be of more help. I can call you if any guides become available if you like."

"Yes please do. We will be at the Golden Sun Hotel." Riccardo said as he picked up his bag and took Crystal's hand.

"Very well senor." The clerk said as they walked away.

Inside their newly booked hotel room Riccardo flopped on

the bed. "I can't believe it, to be so close, only to be stopped by *this*. We don't dare go without an experienced guide."

"Don't worry I am sure they will find someone. No one down here is going to want to turn away money if they can help it."

Riccardo sat up smiling. "You are probably right."

They heard a loud rapping at the door. "Wonder who that could be?" Riccardo said as he stood up.

"A guide perhaps?"

"I don't think so. Not this quick," he said walking to the door. Upon opening it he was greeted by a man with a dark tan of medium height wearing long khaki pants, shirt, and hiking boots. All had seen better days.

"Senor Marino?" The man said with a thick Spanish accent. "The travel company sent me. I am Valdez. I hear you want to go to Angel Falls? Yes?"

"Yes we do but right at the base, up close."

"Can be danger, much water falling now."

"Well we don't need to get that close. But we need to be at the base. I thought no one was available for a few days?"

"That is true senor. But I was on holiday. They called. Told me you might be willing to pay more? Yes?"

"Yes I am. If you are the man for the job."

"I am senor, no one knows the falls better than Valdez." He said tapping his chest. "When you wish to go?"

"Right now if you are available."

"I am senor. Do you have stuff? Food? Ready for long walk? It take time."

"Yes we have everything we need, except for a guide to the area. But I think we just found that," Riccardo smiled.

"Very good senor," Valdez said "I is ready. I have boat. My car below. We go now?"

"Yes, we will get our bags and meet you downstairs."

"Very good senor. I see you soon." Valdez said as he walked away and Riccardo closed the door.

Riccardo turned to Crystal. "Very interesting turn of events. You heard all of that?"

"Yes I did. What do you make of it?" Crystal said.

"He did have the proper information and identification. And often guides freelance around here only being called when a tour is lacking in some area. It is nothing unusual." Riccardo shrugged. "Okay pack up, we are heading out." He said placing the few items he had pulled out back in his bags.

A few moments later they were in Valdez's car heading towards a small airport. "So why you go to Angel floor? Not much to see there," Valdez said over his shoulder.

"Oh, we want to go where most tours don't take you," Riccardo said.

"I see. That true, not many go there. Most don't like get wet. Better view from away too," Valdez said with a smile. "We be at boat in a few minutes."

"Does he seem a bit too chatty?" Crystal whispered.

"Perhaps, but he is trying to make small talk. A guide can be better if they know their clients. I wouldn't worry about it," Riccardo whispered back.

"You're probably right," Crystal sighed.

A few hours and a short flight later Crystal gripped her stomach as the boat pounded up and down against the water. Her stomach got a mind of its own almost as soon as they got on the old tub. "Is it always like this?" She shouted over the roar of the rapids and the boat's engine.

"No," Valdez shouted back, "is often worse!" He chuckled. "Other side of Angel is far worse. You lucky we had lots of rain last week. Would shake more then." He laughed again. "We be there soon."

"Oh?" Riccardo said. "I thought we could see it from this distance."

"Yes, but clouds heavy today. But might see something after we turn around bend," Valdez said with a smile. "You bring cam-a? Yes?"

"Cam-a?" Riccardo said blinking. "Oh camera! Yes we did. Thanks for the reminder." Riccardo said pulling out a digital camera from its waterproof bag just as they cleared the bend in the river and Angel Falls came into view. It was breathtaking. Thousands of gallons of water cascading down like hair from an angel into a misty haze below. "Crystal look!" Riccardo said pointing. Several rainbows could be seen from their position and Riccardo's camera clicked over and over as he took photos.

With the slowing of the water, so had Crystal's stomach, and she forced herself to look up. "Amazing!" she said breathless which could have been from her stomach or the view. "I had always heard about it, and seen pictures, but they pale in comparison to ... to ... this!" She waved her hand over the magnificent vista before them.

"Yes," Valdez said. "You people always say same thing. Valdez knows, has seen much. Still, good to see." He grinned and his grip tightened on the boat's controls. "Where is you want to go now?"

"Can we go to the base of the falls?" Riccardo said pointing.

"Yes. Why you want to go there? Very wet there. No one goes there."

"Well, we want to," Riccardo said.

"Okay, we go there then. You is boss. Hope you have rain stuff," Valdez said laughing.

The river here was as smooth as glass. Crystal looked over the edge but this time not from sickness. She saw several fish swim by. "Oh I just saw some fish, looks like I could reach out and touch them." She said reaching towards the water.

Valdez moved towards her and grabbed her hand. "You not want to that."

"Why not?" Crystal blinked in surprise.

"Vish here eat you. Caribes, very very dangerous." Valdez said releasing her hand and going back to steering the boat.

"Caribes? What are Caribes?"

"Piranha. In Venezuela they are called Caribes." Riccardo said "I didn't realize they were in this part of the river though."

"Yes you call Piranha. Listen to Valdez do not put anything in water you want to get back the same," he said smiling. "Yes they are here. They are everywhere. But we are okay in boat. Have no fear." He pointed to the base of the falls. "We be there soon."

A short time later they were very close to the falls. The roar of the falling water was deafening. "Can we get closer?" Riccardo shouted.

"This not close enough? Is bad idea to go closer." Valdez shouted back.

"Just a little more?" Riccardo shouted again.

Valdez sighed. "Okay little more. But not risking boat for this. The water get hard here." He shouted fighting the boat's wooden wheel as it threatened to spin wildly out of control. A few moments later, the wheel again jarred Valdez, and he fought back. "Okay!" He shouted. "We go no more!"

The water spray had drenched them all and they couldn't hear anything beyond the roar of the falls. The damp smell swirled around them thick with the scents of mold and moss overwhelming their noses. Riccardo moved closer to Crystal and said in her ear. "I don't see anything here do you?"

"No, me either." Crystal said turning back to Riccardo after looking around. "What did that tablet say again?"

"It said to seek between to the pillars letting the setting sun guide us, but I don't see any pillars," Riccardo sighed.

"We go back now, yes?" Valdez shouted.

"A few more minutes." Riccardo shouted back.

"Okay. But sun is setting, we need to make camp soon," Valdez shouted.

"Look!" Crystal said then indicated with her elbow. "Do you see it?"

"See what?" Riccardo said looking around.

"Those two peaks of mountains could be pillars and the sun is about to set between them."

"You are right!" Riccardo said as the sun gently kissed the position between the two mountains. A narrow beam of light shown down to the valley below on the other side of the falls then faded from existence a few seconds later.

"Okay, we are done here," Crystal shouted to Valdez. "Can we go over there and make camp?"

Valdez had already turned the boat around and was heading out under full power. The boat rocked under the strain. Once the fall's roar had diminished he turned. "Over there? Why? Nothing there."

"Well it would be a great place to watch the falls," Crystal said sweetly.

"Yes that true. And we need make camp. Okay we go there," he said smiling.

About thirty minutes later they were setting up camp on the opposite shore that was nestled in-between two large mountain ranges, still soaked from the falls.

"I hope you brought dry clothes and netting," Valdez said. "Very bad to stay wet all night."

"We did, and we brought netting as well." Riccardo said as they continued to unpack.

"Netting?" Crystal asked.

"Mosquito netting."

"Ohh yes we did bring that."

"That is good." Valdez said. "The bugs very bad here. Eat you alive at night without good net."

After camp was set up and a meal of freeze-dried rations later, Crystal snuggled up close to Riccardo under the mosquito netting and whispered in his ear. "I think we need to get rid of our 'guide'."

Riccardo blinked in the firelight. "Why?"

"I don't know, call it a feeling. And with all that we have been through, can you blame me?"

"No, I can't. But I don't know how we are going to 'get rid of' him'."

"I mean he shouldn't be around when we go looking in the morning."

"That is easier said than done. He is our guide, we hired him to be around and stay close. Not to mention it is obvious he knows the area well."

Crystal smiled. "Leave that to me. I have an idea."

Riccardo smiled back. "Oh you do? Care to tell me?"

"Not now ... perhaps later." She winked as she pulled him closer and they drifted off to sleep.

Crystal stretched under the net as the sun's morning rays gently glittered off the Falls. It was not one of the best nights she had ever spent. The camping mats they had bought were lightweight and easily packable, but didn't rate high in comfort. She rubbed a sore shoulder as she sat up. She was tempted to get out her mirror but knew the view would be better unseen. Valdez was already awake making coffee. "Oh good you awake. Well if you aren't, a cup of Valdez's coffee will." He smiled passing her a cup.

"How could I stay asleep with this wonderful smell wafting through the air?" Crystal said taking in the waking aroma emanating from her cup then looked around. "Where is Riccardo?"

"Oh, he is behind the tree. Think my coffee got him." Valdez said laughing just as Riccardo stepped into view.

"Yes it did. You make a really potent brew," he said sitting down.

"My coffee is well-known." Valdez said tapping his chest. "I am more known for coffee being guide." He laughed again.

Crystal sipped the dark drink and while strong it was one of the best cups she had in a long time. "It's very good," she said smiling, "thank you."

"You welcome," he said pouring Riccardo another cup.

"Valdez, how far is the next camp from here?" Crystal asked.

"Hmmm thirty minutes down river. Indian camp. Why?"

"Well do you think they would have insect repellent?"

"Insoct replleont?" Valdez said blinking.

"Yes like this." Crystal said tossing him an empty bottle.

Valdez looked at it then his eyes lit up. "Ohhh this bug stuff. Yes they have this."

"Good, can you go get me some?" Crystal blinked and smiled sweetly.

"Why? We be leaving soon."

"Well I ran out and I need more. Please?" Crystal's smile deepened, and she blinked several more times.

"Well I ...I ...I don't know. I shouldn't leave you here," Valdez stammered.

"Pleeeease? I don't want to be all bug bites and itch for days. I will be fine. Riccardo will be here and we will be safe in this rock corner." Crystal said with the sweetest look she could manage.

"Okay okay. Valdez get you more bug juice," he said smiling. "I will be back soon." He hopped aboard his boat and pulled up the anchor. A few moments later he was around the bend and out of sight.

"Remind me never to play poker with you," Riccardo smiled.

"You never know. It could be fun," Crystal said patting his leg. "Shall we start looking?"

"I thought you already knew since you pointed out the location between the mountains." Riccardo said as his grin widened.

"Well I am guessing by that big tree at the edge of the jungle? And weren't you looking over there earlier?"

"I wondered if you would figure that out. Yes I did, but I didn't see anything."

"Well let's take another look," Crystal said rising to her feet. A moment later they were examining the largest tree in the area. Old enough to have started growing in Atlantis' time, or at least part of it. But they looked all over and didn't find anything unique other than it being incredibly large.

"I don't understand, we were led here but I don't find ...whoooh." Crystal yelled as she went down.

"Are you okay?"

"Yes I am fine." She said while rubbing her foot. "Tripped on a root I guess."

"Hmm there is something under this part of the tree."

Riccardo said pulling at the long root system. With all the recent rain it shifted easily. "Well I'll be. It is another tablet. I bet this tree is the reason no one had found it until now. Good thing we did. In a few more years it would have been impossible to find."

"Well don't stand there with your mouth open. What does it say?"

Riccardo smiled in Crystal's direction then gazed back at the stone slab. "It says something about 'when the sun and moon are at opposites all will be revealed'."

"That is odd."

"No kidding."

"It doesn't say anything else?"

"Not at all."

"Are you sure?"

"Yes. There are a couple of odd circles though, but they don't translate."

"Odd circles?"

"Yes. One large one smaller." Riccardo said looking again at the odd inscriptions.

"Let me see." Crystal said walking over to get a better look. When she looked at the stone tablet, it was obvious it was far larger than what they were seeing. This was only the very top part. "You know," she said taking a deep breath, "if I didn't know better, I would say those two circles look as if they could move."

"Move? What do you mean?" Riccardo said as he stood up getting out of her way.

"Well, let me try something." She reached down and put one finger into one of them and the indention moved slightly. "Ah, I thought so. They are controls of some sort."

"You are right, but they look like normal stone inscriptions. Amazing."

"I'm sure that was the idea," Crystal said with a smile. "What did it say again?"

"When the sun and moon are opposite all will be revealed." Riccardo said with a shrug. "Which doesn't make sense, the sun and moon are always opposite."

"Well not quite, but most of the time yes. Hmm I wonder . . . " Crystal said her voice trailing off as she inserted a finger into each of the circular indentations and pushed. With a little effort they began to slide on a circumference giving a girding sound that emanated deep below them. "Yes, this stone is definitely larger than what we see," she said continuing to push until the two circles were even with each other but on opposite horizontal sides of the tablet. "Well so much for that idea," she said sighing. Then her eyes went wide. "Oh of course!"

"What? I know when you give that look, you are on to something," Riccardo grinned.

Crystal smiled back. "Give me a sec, I might be." She said sticking fingers back into the circles and pushing again this time until they were opposite but vertical with the larger one at the top of the tablet. Just as she got them in position a large click was heard. She looked up. "Well that did a whole lot of good didn't–" A loud growl emanated from deep below them, then the earth shook knocking them off their feet. They scrambled back as they heard grating sounds as though a large machine-in bad need of oil-had been given life. The shaking intensified, and they both moved back a bit more.

The tablet began to rotate counterclockwise, faster and faster. Then it grew, sliding upwards towards the sun. Taller and taller as it was pushed further towards the sky by a stone cylinder below it. Dust and dirt flowed off of every indentation in the otherwise perfect stone creating a cloud around them. When it finally stopped, it was over seven feet tall. There was no doubt it was ancient, yet it hummed with the feeling of something not of this world.

"Now that is not what I expected." Crystal said taking a step closer then stopped as they heard a large bang, a pop, and part of the cylinder slid down revealing an opening. Crystal took another step closer and peered inside seeing a great stone spiral staircase descending deep into the earth below them.

"Nor was I," Riccardo said. "Amazing, so old yet fully functional." He grabbed his pack pulling out a flashlight. "Shall we?"

"Just try to stop me," Crystal said with a wink.

34

What does this say? Crystal asked pointing to the odd inscriptions around the cylinder's doorway.

"As far as I can tell it says 'Welcome to those who seek Sitnalta but be cautious.'" Riccardo said as they entered and began to descend the ancient stone steps.

"A warning? What for?"

"I don't know, but we will keep our eyes open. For all we know they are saying don't run down the steps."

Crystal laughed then heard an odd sound. "Was that you?"

"No. I thought it was you." Riccardo said as he shone the light around landing on where they had came just as the door began to slid back up into place. "The door is closing! That probably means–" They began to feel the shaking again and the walls started to spin. "*Run!* Or we will be crushed!" Riccardo shouted.

They ran down the steps as the walls continued to spin. They could feel the stairs collapsing under their feet. Seconds seemed like hours. Finally, Riccardo's light shone upon a doorway at the bottom of the cylinder. They drove through it as the rest of the staircase closed behind them.

"Well there must be a way to activate the stairs from down

here. We just need to find it." Crystal said while looking at the stone wall behind them that was stairs only a moment ago.

"One would think so." Riccardo said gazing down the large stone hallway they now found themselves in. "I guess we go this way."

"Obviously. What are these?" She said indicating the odd globular structures every few feet along the wall.

"Lights perhaps?" Riccardo said taking a closer look. "Although I don't see any power source and they look like they are solid stone."

"Very strange. And I don't see a light switch."

"Me either." Crystal said as she ran her fingers along the dark wall. It was smooth and exquisitely crafted. She had never seen stone work so perfect. There was not a blemish or signs of construction and looked almost as though they had been placed yesterday. Down the corridor they found doors with what looked like control panels beside them, but nothing happened when the buttons were pressed. "Why did the staircase work and these don't?" Crystal muttered as they walked.

"Perhaps a malfunction? They are very old," Riccardo shrugged.

Crystal shook her head. "But everything here looks as though it was built yesterday. I doubt that."

"Yes you have a point," Riccardo said as they neared the end of the long corridor. One door was far larger than the others but still refused to open when its panel was touched. "Hmm even this one refuses to open. Why doesn't anything work down here?"

"I don't know ... but this one slid open." Crystal pointed at the small doorway at the very end of the hallway now open in front of her. "It didn't have a panel, I just stuck my fingers into this recess and it slid open."

"That is unusual. You would think they would design them all the same." Riccardo said peering inside. "More stairs. I would normally say let's avoid these based on what we just went through. But since we have no other place to go ... " He pointed to them and winked. "Ladies first."

"Gee thanks." She snorted and began climbing. After some time and countless stairs they reached the top, revealing a small room. In the middle of the floor was a carving in the shape of a flower with petals extending all different directions. Along the far wall was a table type shape built into the floor with an odd console on it. The console consisted of a control panel with stone keys.

Riccardo stepped behind the console and studied the keys for a moment. "From what I can tell it talks about how the sun always lights the way."

"Lights the way? Must mean something more than the obvious, judging by what we have seen so far." Crystal shone her light on the panel so Riccardo could study it in more detail.

"I think that some of this is instructions." He said pointing to the side areas. "Hmmm, it talks about first opening the flower, then the window, then something about raising the collector."

"Collector? Window? There is not any window here." Crystal said waving her arm along the stone walls.

"I know. But do we have a choice other than to try it?"

Crystal sighed. "No we don't."

"Okay here goes nothing." Riccardo said as he engaged the first sequence. They felt the floor vibrate as the stone shaped etching began to change ... shifting ... opening up and creating a large star shaped hole revealing a golden shaped dish at the bottom with a huge ruby colored gem at its center. It must have weighed far more than both of them combined. Their flashlights glinted off of its carefully crafted facets reflecting rainbows on the other side of the room.

"Wow," Crystal breathed, "have you ever seen a gemstone that large?"

"Not in one piece. Let alone perfectly crafted. Amazing. Well, let's see what this does." Riccardo said as he engaged the second sequence. The other wall began to shift and move as stones pushed in, then slid down revealing a window. Light streamed in as they both gasped.

"Amazing, we are high above the river in the opposite cliff face. And I can see the falls from here," Crystal said. "I wonder what the last sequence does."

"Let's find out," Riccardo said as he keyed it in. They felt slight tremors in the floor and gazed out the window in time to see a giant stone pillar rise up. It stood three stories tall and of the same expert stone craftsmanship, except for several horizontal rings, at regular intervals, indenting its otherwise smooth surface. They heard a sound emanating from the pillar as gaps appeared along each ring, then the rings spread out and telescoped down revealing two large horizontal panels.

"I wonder what they are for?" Crystal wondered as she pointed at the panels.

"I think we are about to find out." As they watched, the two large panels unfolded further like a giant flower opening. They could hear the loud click as the panels locked into place, then turned as though trying to face the sun. Suddenly, a large beam of energy reflected into the room and bounced into the center of the floor. The giant ruby colored stone glowed brighter and brighter. A few moments later the control panel lights flickered into existence as the strange globe shaped objects outside the room powered on bathing the hallway in an orange glow. Sitnalta had awakened from its long slumber.

35

"Amazing." Crystal said as the orange glow globes continued to brighten further, illuminating the spiral stairs leading down just outside the room. "The city appears to be powered by a solar collector."

"Not just a solar collector. But a solar reactor."

Crystal cocked an eyebrow and looked at Riccardo. "A solar reactor?"

"Yes. A solar collector simply collects the sun's energy as is and stores it for later use. Which is what we do now. But a solar reactor not only collects but makes the energy react in a way that intensifies it. Similar to what a nuclear reactor does, but without the side effects. Of course in this case only true power is generated instead of massive heat as in one of our nuclear reactors." Riccardo pulled out his laptop and plugged in an electronic sensor of some sort into the data port. "This is unbelievable. Judging by the fields this is putting off, this system is producing more energy than a thousand of our nuclear reactors!"

"A thousand?" Crystal blinked while looking at Riccardo's computer. "That can't be right."

"But it is." Riccardo said pointing to his screen. "See here? This indicator proves it. One of these could power a country, more like half of the world.

"This city doesn't seem that large. Why would they need such a vast amount of power?"

Riccardo shrugged. "Who knows, perhaps they planned on expanding later. Or they wanted to build one and not have to worry. It certainly would be a nice feeling never having to worry about running out of power."

"We should go try the other doors. Now that there is power, I bet they will work." Crystal said walking towards the doorway and the staircase.

"I agree. I'll be right there. I want to run one more quick test." He said as his fingers flew over the laptop's keyboard.

"Okay. Don't be too long," Crystal said smiling.

Riccardo looked up and grinned. "La Mia Signora, you know I can't stay away from you for long."

Crystal walked down the stairs to the main hallway. She decided these doors must lead to the rest of the city but wondered which door to try first. Then her gaze fell upon the largest one. "This one." She thought as she reached for the stone panel alongside the door, which was now illuminated with a faint blue glow. She pushed one button, but nothing happened. Then she tried another but the door still refused to respond. She began to think, "I should have waited for Riccardo, he could read these markings." Crystal turned to leave when the large stone door slid open revealing a great chamber beyond. The light globes were still dim here, no doubt the reactor had not recharged the city quite yet.

She stepped inside and the lights started to brighten. She took another hesitant step, and the door snapped shut behind her. Crystal spun around in a blur of motion. "Riccardo?" she called.

A man stepped out from the shadows and leveled a pistol

in Crystal's direction. "He is no here." Valdez said with a grin large enough to swallow an oil tanker whole.

"Valdez! What's going on?"

"You can drop the pretense, I know you know."

"Know what?" Crystal blinked.

Valdez took his other hand and with a deft motion wiped makeup from his face then pulled off a facial appliance. "This!"

Crystal's mouth hung open for a second and she forced it closed only to open it again to exclaim "Agent Mighcrow!"

"Correct. And may I say you play the shocked innocent woman very well."

"Who is pretending?" Crystal said rolling her eyes.

"Don't play coy with me. I know you knew who I was. Or you wouldn't have sent me off on a wild goose chase. Or tried to. At least now I don't have to speak with limited intelligence and vocabulary." Mighcrow said while resting himself against the now closed doorway.

"Why are you doing this? I thought you were with the government?"

"I am. Well actually, I am with whoever pays the most. Officially I am Agent Mighcrow. Unofficially I am the one that people pay when they want difficult jobs done. I learned long ago I could either continue to work for our government and probably die at a young age or even if I lived, to retire with a pittance of a pension. Or I could take my considerable talents to the market and be paid well for my trouble. I chose the latter," he said as his grin widened.

"You have been working for Benton all this time?" Crystal's mouth to hung open again for a moment before she forced it closed.

"No. When we first met I was on official business. Later,

Benton called, and I happened to be there anyway, which turned out to be very advantageous. He pays very well for my services. Of course he has to, if he wants things done properly," Mighcrow chuckled. "I have to admit though, it is rare for someone to keep ahead of me as you have. I am paid to be one step ahead, not two steps behind. If it wasn't for that button tracker, I never would have found you in Venezuela. Did you forget about it?" Crystal's eyes widened. "I figured you did. Still, you are to be commended."

"Gee thanks, I will make sure to put it on my resume," Crystal snorted.

"This is quite the find, and I have you to thank for it. I know this will make me very rich." Mighcrow said as he walked around the large circular room they found themselves in. Always making sure to keep the gun pointed in Crystal's direction.

"You're welcome." Crystal said through gritted teeth. "So glad we could oblige. And how did you get down here?"

"Riccardo is not the only one that can read Ancient Greek my dear. I will admit it was not easy figuring out that spiral staircase, but I had seen it come up. With that knowledge, it simplified the situation."

"You were watching us?"

"Of course."

"But we saw you leave."

"It's what I wanted you to see. Right after I was out of sight, I put out my anchor and made my way back the short distance along the very edge of the river in time to see you activate the staircase." Mighcrow smiled walking closer to Crystal who was now standing near one of the large control consoles in the odd room. "And now you have run me a merry chase ... but it's over."

"Are you going to shoot me?" Crystal said glaring.

"My dear, that might damage this fine room and my profits. I wouldn't dream of it." He said pulling out a flashlight. Pushing a switch on the bottom caused two metal points to sick out. "This might look like a common stun gun but I have modified it. On the highest setting it should take care of the situation and without damage to this fine equipment."

Crystal saw electricity arcing between the contact points. She sighed and held up her hands as he took the final step closer, reaching out with the stunner. She dove towards Mighcrow knocking the stunner out of his one hand and fighting for the gun in the other.

Riccardo stared at the door. He saw it open and Crystal enter, but it now refused to budge. While the panel's lights were on, it seemed to be locked from the inside. "Crystal!" He shouted but there was no answer and realized the walls must be soundproof. Then an idea hit him, there must be another way in. It is doubtful a city of such complexity would only allow one entrance into a room. Especially one with such a large door.

He ran for the next door which opened with ease revealing another hallway similar to the one he was in. The light globes lit the long corridor with their orange glow. Here as everywhere the impressive stone construction stood as a testament to its incredible builders. The door control panels were active and lit, but they still refused to open. Near the end of the corridor he found one that slid open with some coaxing to reveal another hallway similar to the first. Riccardo began to think these builders had a secret maze fetish.

Running down the hall, he found another door in the middle. He made a quick calculation in his head and thought this door must be heading in the direction of the room Crystal was in. The door didn't open at first, but then he realized the keypad was asking a question instead of being a simple open and close control. Apparently there was some damage and it was asking if it wanted him to attempt self-repair. He keyed in his agreement and the door hummed, then slid open.

What he saw filled him with horror. A man in Valdez's clothes, yet wasn't him, was fighting with Crystal. A gun wielded between them. While neither was giving in, he knew that she couldn't hold out against this man for much longer. He wanted to run to Crystal but if he did, the distraction might turn the tide against her. He slipped inside, making sure not to be seen, yet moving as fast as he could. The large circular room was full of equipment and control panels which made it easy for him to hide his approach. But when he got close enough to make his move, the tide had turned.

The man hit Crystal on the head with the gun and she crumpled to the floor behind a large stone table. Then he raised his gun preparing to finish the job. "Crystal!" Riccardo shouted. The man looked up his eyes wide and raised his gun. Riccardo grabbed the large survival knife at his left hip and hurled it towards the man in one fluid motion. The man tried to react. Too late. The knife reached its target and dove straight into the man's eye and into his brain. Blood gushed from the wound and his other eye rolled back as he collapsed to the floor.

36

"Very good! I didn't think you had it in you!" Benton stood clapping before two large columns in the center of the room pointing his gun at Riccardo. "Where is the woman?"

"Her name is Crystal," Riccardo said turning around.

"All right, where is Crystal?" Benton sneered.

"Your minion killed her!" Riccardo exclaimed.

"Why do I doubt you? Although my men are very efficient when properly directed. Which is why I never could trust this …" He paused to wave his gun around the chamber. "To just them. I had to be here, to claim my prize."

Riccardo looked around. "Only you? Where are the rest?"

"Oh they will be here soon enough. I needed to get here fast, and that is very expensive."

"Since when do you have money problems?"

"*That* is none of your concern! And shall be rectified shortly once I sell the technology here. I never dreamed Croorlheart's discovery was all of … this." Benton gestured around the room again with his gun. "I knew it would be worth a kings ransom, but this is more like having the world in the palm of your hand! Thank you for handing it to me. I don't know if I could have found it without you."

"Did you have to kill him? He didn't do you any harm."

"Ah but he *did!* He betrayed me! And after all the resources I gave him. This discovery was paid for by me! If it wasn't for me, we would not be here now. And for all of that, he betrayed me and tried to give it to you."

"Only after he found out who you really–"

"Silence! At least I not only get my prize ... but to put you out of my misery." He said leveling his gun in Riccardo's direction. "It's a shame, I hate to waste such a talent. But business is business." His finger tightened on the trigger.

Crystal pulled herself up to the table ... no ... console in front of her. She fought to clear her blurred vision. Her head throbbed from where Mighcrow had struck her. She stared at the panel. It was full of stone buttons. Some lit by a strange glow. Others very dark. Her vision blurred again, and she shook her head to try to clear it, which was a mistake. "OW," she grunted under her breath. She could hear Benton and Riccardo's argument which was growing louder and knew they wouldn't be talking for much longer. She pushed herself up a little more and could see them standing over by the large twin columns.

Crystal lowered herself back down and looked at the panel again wishing she took Greek instead of French in high school. Then it hit her, the glowing buttons were in an odd pattern. She looked up then back realizing that they were laid out in a diagram indicating the different parts of the chamber.

"It's a pity you never would join me. You would have been a valuable asset," Benton sneered. "Goodbye Riccardo Marino, you led me a long chase but it's now over." He raised the pistol and his finger tensed on the trigger.

Crystal was out of time. She held her breath and pushed a button in the center of the diagram and silently prayed. It lit up and began to glow brighter than the others. Sparks began to fly from other areas in the room.

Benton's eyes grew wide. "What have you done?"

Riccardo shook his head and held up his hands. "I didn't do anything!"

"Yooohooooo." Crystal called as she pushed herself up and waved.

Benton whirled around. "YOU!" He shouted as he aimed towards her squeezing the trigger. But the shot never happened.

A giant energy bolt lashed out from one pillar to the other reaching right through Benton. He gasped with pain as the power grew in intensity lifting him up off of the ground into the exact center of the two columns. Then another bolt struck him from the top of the other pillar and grew brighter. Two more bolts came up from the base on either side and merged with the first two. Benton howled as a giant crack was heard shaking the whole complex. He shouted "NOOOOOOO!" as a warp in space formed in his middle filling the room with the smell of ozone. The spacial rift expanded causing Benton to evaporate in a puff of black smoke. The warp continued to grow until it filled the space between the two columns. The ancient Door of Atlantis was now open.

Suddenly the air was filled with the smell of sulfur and air rushed into The Door knocking Riccardo off of his feet. The Door had taken on an angry red-orange hue as its pull increased. He grabbed one of the stone steps leading up to the columns to stop himself from being sucked in. "Shut it off!" he shouted.

Crystal pressed the same button as before over and over again. "It's not working!" The air swirled with dust and debris being sucked into The Door. She knew it was only a matter of time before Riccardo followed them.

"I can't hold on!" he shouted. "I am slipping!" His grip gave out sending him hurtling towards The Door. At the last second he managed to grab a cable that was still attached to a console. He felt like a rock climber in a hurricane as he was held out horizontally from the ground as The Door as it tried to suck him in. "Crystal!" He shouted again as the cable started to fray.

Crystal looked down at the panel. "Which one?" she thought. Perhaps the button from before was a 'ON' and another is 'OFF'. She looked around the panel. "It must be here somewhere," she muttered.

"Crystal!" Riccardo shouted again. His sweaty hands had slipped more, and the cable frayed threatening to break any second.

Crystal looked over the panel again and noticed one button that wasn't glowing before. She closed her eyes praying as she pressed it. It felt as if they entered the eye of a storm. The air stopped swirling around and items started falling to the ground with a large *thud*. The giant electrical bolts that had sustained The Door shrank in size and disappeared taking the warp in space with them.

"*Ow!*" Riccardo said as he hit the ground. "It sure took you long enough!"

Crystal ran over to him. "Hey, you are the one with the ancient Greek. You are lucky I figured out there was a separate button for OFF and it wasn't glowing before. Are you okay?" she said feeling his shoulder.

"Ow! Yes if you stop squeezing there," he said with a smile.

"Well at least your humor is still with us." She playfully slapped his other shoulder.

Riccardo sat up and held her tight. "I thought I had lost you." He kissed her lips.

Crystal kissed him back. "And I almost lost you. Don't ever do that again."

Riccardo chuckled. "Don't worry I won't."

She sat down alongside of him. "What do we do now?"

"Well, I will get a team together to study this city."

"I suspect your stock prices just went through the roof."

He laughed. "No, only to learn and then we release it to the world. They left this here for everyone. Besides, it is what Terrance wanted."

"Looks like we have a lot of work to do then."

"We?"

"Well you don't think I would leave you alone to this whole huge thing do you?" Crystal smiled taking his hands into hers.

"What about your job? Your life?"

"You are my life, now."

Riccardo squeezed her hand tightly. "And you are mine ... I ... I ... Love You." He blurted out finally realizing it. For the first time in his life he felt true love.

"And I love you." She kissed him passionately while thinking Mia was never going to believe this one.

About The Author

Don DeBon is the author of numerous science fiction novels and short stories. Don lives in USA where he continues to dream up more fantastic worlds for you to enjoy. When not writing, he can usually be found devouring another science fiction book, TV series, or movie.

Some of his latest work include:

Red Warp

In a race against time the casualty could be your life.

If you could travel through time with just yourself and no machine needed, would you?

Meet Red, a woman with a amazing gift, the gift of passing though time and space without the need of any bulky equipment. The places she has seen, the people she has helped will blow your mind.

Now meet James, just your average newly minted FBI agent minding his own business until he is thrust headlong into Red's world. A world he didn't ask for, but one that hit him in the face full force. Can they get along long enough to survive?

Time Rock

Time Travel. Blessing or curse? One man thinks he has it all figured out but what began as a simple test has turned into a nightmare. With his equipment failing all around him, only Red and James can save him. Can they reach him in time?

Soulmates

Mechands . . . everyone has one. The metal race built by man to serve our every need. But Aleshia is about to find out they are not the benevolent protectors that she has always been taught. And who is this strange man in her dreams? The man who actually exists and reveals the whole world is not as she thought.

Word of mouth is crucial for authors. If you enjoyed this book, would you consider leaving a review? It is very much appreciated.

Amazon USA
http://www.amazon.com/

Amazon UK
http://www.amazon.co.uk/

Goodreads
http://www.goodreads.com

Connect with the Author
Email: writer.don.debon@gmail.com
Mailing List: http://eepurl.com/bxWAov
Website: http://www.dondebon.com
Twitter: @DonDeBon
Google+: +DonDeBon

This Edition Published 2018 by
DBDigital Publishing

ISBN 978-0-9881783-1-1
ISBN 978-0-9881783-0-4 (e-book)